The Submissive's Touch

Love in the Shadows

Book 1

By

Abby Gordon

Contents

Chapter One

The bed shuddered and Ally whimpered in her sleep, burrowing into her pillow. The images flashed into her mind. *Dark night, Grandpa Mack and Uncle Jack laughing, Mom shaking her head at the two of them. The bright headlights. Her shock as Uncle Jack tried to turn the car.* At the loud boom and the window shaking again, Ally sat bolt upright in bed, gasping for air. Her body was covered in sweat. *Just a dream. No, not a dream. The past. A past I can't change.* Crying, Ally curled on the bed.

She remembered nothing more about the accident that had changed her life. That had taken the lives of her family. Until she'd woken four days later in the hospital to see two strangers at her bedside. Until she'd been told that her father had not just been Tom Brown, but Thomas David Brown the Fifth who had been disowned by his father, the Fourth, for refusing to marry the woman the Fourth had selected. A legal firm had been hired to track and keep tabs on him. By chance a friend of her cousin's, son of her father's younger brother, had overheard the conversation between partners and called David.

Even as he'd tried to unravel the deception, David and his English born wife Lady Diana Willoughby had raced to Maine to be with her. When she'd recovered enough to be moved, they'd brought her to their NYC penthouse.

Smiling now against the pillow, Ally recalled David's story of the previous evening. He'd been waging a not-so silent war against those who had kept their grandfather's secret. The law firm was taking a huge PR hit and losing several top clients. Ally had done what she could to help, sending for her father's papers. Tom Brown's diaries and the returned letters had given evidence when the lawyers had tried to deny knowledge.

Realizing she was now too awake to fall back asleep, Ally eased her legs, just freed ten days earlier from their casts, over the edge of the bed. A hand on the nightstand helped her balance as she stood up. Letting go, she waited, then grinned when she didn't topple over.

"Progress, Ally," she praised herself. "A day at a time."

Slowly, she went to the window, hoping the weather forecast of clear skies was holding. Diana had convinced David to leave the office so they could picnic in Central Park. Ally was looking forward to being able to explore the city without being limited by her crutches.

Pulling open the drapes, she stared in uncomprehending horror. *I'm seeing this. This cannot be real.* She rubbed her eyes and looked again. Whirling and stumbling for the door, she tried to understand what she'd seen – *what could cause a fire like that?* Turning the knob, she was shouting even as she pulled it open.

"David! Diana!

Both appeared from the direction of the kitchen. David sprinted ahead of his waddling wife. "Ally, are you okay? Is it your legs?"

"The World Trade Center," she gasped. "It's on fire."

"What?" he caught her shoulders, holding her steady. "What are you talking about?"

"One of the towers is burning," she told him as Diana reached them. Grabbing at his shirt with one hand, she waved across the room with the other. "At first I thought it was a dream about the crash . . ." She started crying. "There's a huge hole in the side."

He released her and entered her room, crossing to the window. "Oh, my God."

The women joined him and stared at the sight. They all saw it at the same time.

"Is that . . ." Ally whispered.

"What is that pilot . . ." Diana wondered.

"He's aiming . . ." David breathed.

In horror, they watched the plane strike the second tower, lower than the now gaping hole in the first tower. Helplessly, David held both women as none of them could turn away from the horror. Smoke billowed from both buildings.

"Oh, my God," wept Diana. "All those people."

"Why?" Ally asked, looking up at David. "Was there something on the news this morning? Are we at war?"

A shocked, numb expression on his face, David shook his head. "I didn't hear anything while I was shaving," he replied in a strangled voice. "Whether we're at war or not, we've just been attacked."

"But why? By whom?" Diana cried out in fear.

"Mr. Brown? Lady Diana?" called the voice of the housekeeper. "Have you heard?"

Quick footsteps on the parquet could be heard and, as they turned, she appeared at the door. The woman in her mid-thirties was pale from shock.

"A plane hit one of the towers. I saw it after I dropped Marcus off."

Ally caught her breath. Carla's son's elementary school was several blocks away in the opposite direction. Carla would have been able to see it as she returned to the building.

"That boom I heard was the plane hitting the first tower," she breathed.

"You're going to Long Island," David decided firmly. "All of you. Diana, Ally, Carla. You'll pick Marcus up and you'll all go to the house. I don't want any of you in Manhattan."

"David—" his wife and cousin protested together.

"No, dammit," he cut them off. "No arguments. Ally, get dressed. Carla, quickly grab some things for you and Marcus. I want all of you gone in ten minutes."

A hand under Diana's elbow, he guided his wife out of the room, closing the door as he continued to give directions to Carla. Tearing her gaze from the window, Ally pulled the curtains closed and dressed as quickly as she could.

****

Something's wrong. Something is very wrong.

"What's wrong?" his spotter murmured. "Besides the fact that a blind person could have picked off every one of these idiots?"

Despite his disquiet, JW Franklin smiled slightly. A U.S. Army sniper, he and his partner/spotter Parker Black, were participating in an exercise ranging across central Texas.

"Let's see how they react to this," he replied, pulling the trigger, adjusting and pulling several more times.

In the valley below them, the harnesses of four senior officers began to beep.

"Nice shooting," Parker chuckled. "You ever hit someone that high up?"

"Two stars don't usually participate in these shindigs," JW drawled.

"Gee, I wonder why," drawled the spotter.

"I think he's the National Guard general from one of the Dakotas. I've heard they get out of the office more."

"Yeah, I heard he's a rancher," Parker nodded, peering through the glasses to keep tabs on the reaction. "He did react pretty fast to the colonel getting hit though. I'm surprised you got him." He turned and frowned at the sniper. "You're feeling something, aren't you? What is it?"

"I'm not sure," JW admitted. Parker was one of the few who knew of the O'Grady 'talents.' *Just a feeling of fear spreading as fast as flames.* The New York City skyline flashed in his mind. A shiver swept through him. "But something is very wrong."

"I hate it when you get that feeling," muttered Parker. "I really do."

"Ditto."

Their radio crackled.

"Bravo Zulu," the senior command post identified itself. "All units, disengage and report to base. Repeat, all units are to end the exercise and report to base. Sniper teams, report on the double."

Already breaking down their equipment, JW and Parker froze, glanced at the radio then at each other. To interrupt, much less end the exercise, was rare. To specify a certain group? Theirs? JW could think of only one reason.

"Shit hit the fan," Parker put the thought into words.

JW didn't bother to respond. Slinging his rifle, he settled his pack straps on his shoulders and started out at a steady lope. Parker fell into step beside him as, down in the valley, the soldiers were also trotting.

Picked up by a truck sent to gather the teams farthest out, JW and Parker jumped out the back as soon as it stopped in front of the main tent. Two military police sergeants checked their IDs to what they had on their lists.

"Sniper teams are to report to the S2 for intel," one told them. "General Carruthers will brief you."

"What happened?" Parker asked as a dozen more soldiers gathered.

"Planes hit the Twin Towers," a corporal answered.

JW felt his blood freeze as he remembered the image that had flashed in his mind. And flames.

"We've been attacked," he breathed.

"No one's saying that," a nearby major rebuked.

"Give me a fucking break," JW told him. He'd started basic training two days after he'd graduated the elite preparatory school in Connecticut. For more than fourteen years, his mother's family's social status and business dealings had been a distant memory, but now it became the only thing he could think of. *Mom.* Even knowing he was too far away, he tried to reach her mentally. *Nothing. God dammit.* "Oh, shit. Where's a phone? Someone get me a fucking phone!"

"We're under communication blackout," the major told him.

"Major," JW glared at him. "Odds are I've got family, my *mother,* in the Towers right now. I don't care if the *president* ordered comm silence. I'm getting on a phone and—"

"Problem, sergeant?" the two-star general cut in with a hard voice.

JW turned as everyone stiffened to attention. The nametag on the fatigues read Carruthers. *Figures. I shoot the man I may need to help me but will the family mean anything to him?* The general nodded, recognizing both facts without saying a word.

"Sir, my mother's entire family is in New York City. Odds are high that she, my grandfather, an uncle or two, and cousins were in the Towers when the planes hit." He struggled to maintain military discipline as his mind screamed. *Mom? Gisele?* Yet he

11

couldn't reach either of them. His cousin Gisele was one of the strongest empaths in the extended O'Grady family. JW could just imagine what she was going through. *The Towers. Dear God, how many people would be in those two buildings? In the area?*

"I understand your concern, Sergeant Franklin," the general replied in a slightly less harsh tone. "But right now, we have a job to do."

"Yes, sir," JW replied, taking a deep breath and struggling to pull himself together.

"Nice shooting out there by the way," the general told him as he handed his harness to a hovering lieutenant. "Unfortunately, I'm afraid you'll be doing it for real all too soon."

"I've done it before, sir. I have no problem doing it again."

With a nod, the general gestured for the snipers to follow him.

After hours of briefings while trying to follow "fog of war" media reports and the shock of seeing the Towers collapse, the Pentagon hit, and then a fourth plane crashing in Pennsylvania, JW was finally able to get through to the Long Island mansion of his grandparents. One of the staff answered and quickly found his mother.

"Alive. Everyone in the family is alive," Zoey told him without greeting, knowing her son's first concern.

"Thank God," he whispered, letting himself relaxing slightly. Next to him, Parker smiled, gripped his shoulder before walking away. "Oh, thank God."

"Daddy, Jonas, and Grant were in the south tower, but they were below where the plane hit," she elaborated, referring to the oldest of her younger brothers and his oldest son. "They started walking out with David Brown. David's driver brought Diana and his cousin out here and turned around to try to find David. He picked them up halfway. They said it was more chaos than anything they'd ever seen or imagined."

"How bad do you think it will be? How many killed?" JW braced himself.

"I've no idea," she whispered. "Rumors say several thousand couldn't get out. The fire and police departments will be devastated from the losses. So many of them ran in to help the people trapped. So . . . so many."

She was weeping and JW closed his eyes at the sound. He couldn't recall her crying more than once or twice in his childhood.

"Mom," he murmured, not sure what to say.

"You'll be going after them, won't you?" she said quietly. "No, never mind. I don't expect you can answer that. Tell me something. Anything. What have you been up to?"

"We were on an exercise this morning," he replied. "Our target was spread out like a flock of ducks on a perfect afternoon. I picked off the senior officers easily, including a two-star."

He could hear her relaxing by the chuckle.

"Way to impress the higher-ups, love."

"I take after my mother," he drawled.

"God help the Army," she sighed.

"Mom, I love you."

"I love you more," she told him and he could hear her voice tightening with emotion. "Always. And I'm so proud of you. In everything you do."

Chapter Two

That evening convoy of trucks left the central Texas installation and drove nonstop through to the sprawling post in central North Carolina. Upon their arrival, they were told they wouldn't be leaving for thirty hours. JW didn't hesitate after the commander gave them 24-hour liberty and went to a phone.

"Grant, don't ask any questions," he said when his cousin answered. He whispered a code word he'd given him years earlier, praying he'd never have to say it. "Shadows."

"You got it," Grant replied without hesitation, the tapping of his fingers on the keyboard audible over the phone to initiate the plan they'd prepared. "Good thing the ban on flying just got lifted."

The private plane landed at the North Carolina county civilian airport, and JW, still in uniform, climbed aboard as it refueled. Within minutes, the plane was back in the air. Upon landing on an equally small airport on Long Island, the door opened and the attendant lowered the steps, JW smiled for the first time since the attacks. The limousine waited and the chauffer got out, nodding to him before going to the passenger door. To his surprise, it wasn't his cousin who emerged but his mother. Tears in his eyes, he moved quickly but she still beat him to the bottom of the aluminum steps that clanked under his boots.

"Sh," she whispered, hugging him as he reached the bottom. "Just let me hold my baby a moment."

"Mom." *Seriously. Only my mother . . .*

"Hush."

"Yes, ma'am," he sighed, letting himself relax.

"Here you go, Mr. Franklin," the plane's attendant said quietly.

JW turned and realized, in his haste to reach his mother, he had dropped his duffle bag in the plane's doorway.

"Thank you, Stan. Appreciate it."

"Not at all, sir," the man said quietly. "We'll be here when you need us."

Zoey choked back a sob and Stan just nodded at JW and stepped back.

"C'mon, Mom," he said softly, slinging the bag over a shoulder as he guided her back to the car with an arm around her shoulders. "I don't want to spend my time on the tarmac."

"Right," she agreed. "No tears."

"Mom, from you, they're okay," he told her as Johnson took the bag and carried it to the trunk. He ushered his mother into the car and glanced southwest. The towers had once been visible the last time he'd been home. Now, there was only a smoking emptiness. "God damn them all to hell," he muttered.

"Amen to that, sir," Johnson agreed. "Straight home, sir?"

"Straight home," he confirmed, getting in next to his mother.

A few minutes later, they were on the expressway. His mother had recovered most of her composure.

"How bad is it going to be?" he asked quietly.

She understood his meaning and looked up at him with the same eyes he saw in his reflection. Eyes that saw and understood more than most. Her father's mother had been an O'Grady descended from Padraig O'Grady who fled Ireland. He'd used his wits and muscle to have his own pub. His son had added on to the building to create a hotel. The original establishment had become more in the third generation. Padraig's grandson had kept the public side and added to it, creating the Shadows, a safe haven for people to explore their sexual tendencies.

JW hadn't ever let himself consider that his mother knew about that side. But she did know about the rest of Padraig O'Grady's legacy. He had claimed to be the seventh son of a druid. JW didn't quite believe the druid part, but he couldn't deny the rest. Padraig had been gifted with foresight and other mental abilities. While it was mostly the descendants of his oldest son who inherited those gifts, it did appear in others. Zoey was the only one of Hal Franklin's children who had it, and she seemed to have received the portions for herself and her younger siblings. For his generation, JW had enough to call it heightened awareness and, if close enough, pick up the thoughts and feelings of family members. But Gisele and Nick were considerably more gifted. If one could call it that. *On a day like Tuesday* . . .

"It won't be a war like anything else," his mother whispered.

"How are Gisele and Nick?" A college senior, Grant's younger sister Gisele was highly empathic and JW wasn't even sure what to call Nick. *Besides trouble with a capital T.*

His mother closed her eyes.

"Gisele was in class and became hysterical from the pain she felt. I gave her a sedative when she got home. And Nick," she sighed, shaking her head. "God help us with that boy. Sam Hancock called very early Wednesday morning. Nick broke into the headmaster's house and stole two bottles of brandy."

"He didn't?" JW stared at her as she opened her eyes. He could see the emotions—a strange pride at what her nephew had done to deal with what the anguish of the events. Part of him wanted to burst out laughing at what his cousin had done. But part of him ached for what Nick and Gisele had felt. He'd been half way across the country and given some distance. JW didn't want to think about their agonies. *And it wouldn't be over anytime soon.* "He did. And drank it? All of it? Two bottles?"

"Bottle and a half. Sam confessed that he had some, but Nick had most of it," she confirmed with a firm nod. "Adam," she referred to her youngest brother who was Nick's father, "was so furious I'm surprised he wasn't spitting nails. So, I went up with him."

"Uncle Adam would have let it rip without realizing how his words would hurt Nick," JW murmured. He loved his grandmother, but she refused to acknowledge what her daughter or some of her grandchildren could do. His uncles were the same way. "I'll bet that didn't go over well with Nick."

"Not at all," she whispered. "Adam talked nonstop," she stopped and shook her head. "Correction. He *yelled* at Nick nonstop for nearly an hour. Not repeating himself once. Nick was nearly catatonic and unable to explain anything. When Adam finally paused for a breath, I told him to go take the headmaster the two bottles Daddy had sent with us in compensation and that I would talk to Nick."

"Oh, how did you manage that?"

Uncle Adam had difficulty taking direction from nearly everyone around him. JW privately thought it was because he'd been so spoiled growing up.

"I pulled rank on him," she replied calmly with a small satisfied smile.

"You don't do that often," he remarked, letting himself grin at the thought of his uncle's reaction. As the oldest Franklin in her generation, Zoey was positioned higher in the family business than her brothers because of a clause in their great-great-grandfather's trust, and there was still a bit of awe in them for her one rebellion. *Me. She had me and refused to give me up.* "What did he do?"

Shrugging, she waggled her brows.

"He muttered a bit, then left us alone."

"And Nick?" JW wondered. "You took his pain, didn't you?"

Quietly, Zoey simply looked at him.

"He was hungover until this morning." JW snorted at that. *Leave it to Mom to ease part but make sure the lesson is still learned.* "He accepted the three-day suspension and came home with us. He'll need to talk to you."

"I'm not nearly as strong as he is," JW replied with a shake of his head.

"He needs you, JW," she whispered. "You're strong in ways you don't understand or know yet."

That jolted him.

"Mom, what have you seen?"

"You know I don't do that," she scolded.

Scowling, he glared at the tips of his boots. He knew better than to glare at his mother. No matter how old he got, he'd learned young that certain lines not even he could cross with his mother. There weren't many, but some questions she wouldn't answer even if they were his.

"I'll figure I don't die," he murmured. "I don't think you'd be this calm if you'd seen that."

"I'd be more medicated than Gisele," she confirmed in a quiet voice.

"And that's all you'll say."

Her hand reached for him and he grasped it, taking comfort in the touch. For a long moment, they simply stared at each other. Slowly, he felt himself calm and become centered.

"You're doing it again," he chided, yet didn't resist.

She remained silent. With a sigh, he closed his eyes, letting her bring him what peace she could.

***

There was no peace from her when they entered the mansion. JW wisely stepped back after greeting his grandparents. Grant arrived from the office and didn't say a word as he sidled over. Zoey in a temper was something that everyone avoided. She didn't let it rip often at family members, but when she did, no one got in her path. From the left of the entryway they watched Zoey square off against Henrietta. JW hoped he and Grant would be able to signal the younger cousins before they stepped into the line of fire. *Gisele, be careful,* he thought to Grant's younger sister. *Mom and Grandmother are at it in the main hall.*

"Mother, how on earth could you even think of having a party so soon?" she demanded. "My God, there's still smoke coming from the crash sites. They're still trying to determine how many were killed, and you decide to continue with a party?"

"I had no idea Jay would be home," Henrietta huffed. "Perhaps if you weren't so secretive about your son's comings and goings, then the rest of us would be better able to plan."

Zoey lowered her head like a bull getting ready to charge.

"Oh, shit," muttered Grant. "That's so not good."

"Nope," JW agreed as Bron appeared through the front door and suddenly stopped when he saw his grandmother and aunt at the foot of the staircase.

Assessing the situation, he sidestepped over to his cousins.

"What did I miss?" he whispered as Zoey spoke again.

"His name is JW," she ground out. "And if I'm secretive about his comings and goings it's because his job requires it, which you have never even *tried* to understand. And I was not referring to his arrival, Mother."

"You know I don't like it when you call me that," Henrietta snapped at her as Gisele, Nick, Henry, Heather, Penny, and Nora came from the library. One look at the tableau had Gisele, the oldest granddaughter, tugging on sleeves to urge them to join the older three.

"And you know I don't like it when you screw up my son's name," the daughter fired back. "I'm talking about the fact that God knows how many thousands of Americans were killed by enemies of this country and you don't seem to understand that now is not the time to have a fucking party!"

"There is no need for that kind of language, young lady," reprimanded the matriarch. "Jay will have plenty of time over the weekend to cavort about the city with his friends."

"Jesus Christ, Mother," Zoey breathed, so stunned she stepped back. "You really don't get it, do you? The country is at war. My *son* is about to go to war. And he won't be here over the weekend. He's only here a few hours before he has to go back. *And his name is JW*," she snarled.

"What?" Henrietta sent a confused glance to where her grandchildren stood. The younger ones clustered behind the older four. "Don't be silly, Zoey. He's always here for several days. He and Grant can call their friends and have them over tomorrow. It should still be warm enough for a pool party."

Zoey opened and closed her mouth a couple times then sent her father a look that spoke volumes. Although he adored his wife and his first-born daughter, Hal Franklin had not survived as long as he had by getting between them when they argued.

"Daddy, you deal with her," she told him, her voice vibrating with anger. As low as it was, JW could almost feel the echoes bouncing off the wall because of the intensity. "Because if I have to say one more word to her, then I'll fucking destroy everything in my path."

Without another word, she spun on her heel and disappeared into the library. Struggling to contain his own temper, JW met his grandmother's artfully confused and hurt expression with an implacable one of his own.

"Jay, talk to her," the older woman urged. "She's being totally unreasonable. Heavens, swearing like that. Giving me that kind of attitude. I don't understand what's gotten into her." Her dark eyes landed on Gisele and Nick. "Or others in this family."

Stepping ahead of his cousins, JW gathered in all the strength and discipline he'd learned throughout his years in the military and, before that, from his mother.

"Grandmother, pay attention. Pull your head out of your own little bubble." As furious as he was, he wouldn't be so crude as to tell his grandmother to pull her head out of her ass. Even his mother would land on him for that. "I'm only here overnight. I don't know where I'll be in seventy-two hours. I don't know if I'll be alive in a week. *That* is what has gotten into my mother. That is what she is dealing with." He took three steps to follow his mother, then paused and turned to look at the older woman. "And my name is JW."

"Who names their child something like that?" Henrietta demanded, bringing up a debate that had simmered between her and her daughter since JW's birth. "Letters in the alphabet. Absolutely ridiculous. Not even a proper middle name we could use."

"That is what Mom named me. I will not answer to anything else. From *anyone*. Ever again. End of discussion."

Before anyone could say another word, he went into the library and closed the door. His mother stood across the room, gazing out at the landscaped lawn and gardens. At her feet lay the frisbees his younger cousins had been tossing outside and dropped when they'd come inside and heard the argument.

"Mom?"

"I'm sorry about that," she replied, not turning her head. "She seems to rejoice in pushing my buttons and then twisting things so I am in the wrong and should apologize to her."

JW walked across the black walnut floors and Oriental carpet to stand next to her before speaking. "I told her I wouldn't answer to anything but my name again."

"She won't like that," Zoey muttered.

"Sorry if that makes things more difficult for you." He put an arm around her shoulders. "You'll have to deal with her when I leave."

"Sweetheart, you've nothing to be sorry for," she sighed, resting into him. "I'm the one who should apologize to you. God, I've made your entire life difficult because of my choices."

"I'm stronger from it. And I've had your love. Mom . . ." he hesitated, then plunged on. *No matter what she's seen, what I told Grandmother is the truth. I don't know if I'll be alive in a week and I know damn well that uncertainty is eating at her.* His heart full, knowing what she was going through, yet he knew he had to ask questions he hadn't in a couple decades. Something in him needed to know. "Mom, who was my father? Does he know you had me? Why did you name me JW?"

"Sweetheart," she whispered as sorrow spiked in waves from her.

"Please."

Bowing her head, she remained silent a moment. He held his breath.

"His name was Jean, from a French family that goes back to the days of Charlemagne. A wolf's head is on their crest. That's what the JW stands for. Jean Wolf." Her sad eyes met his. "I would tease him about being a wolf. The first couple weeks I was in Paris, it was as if he was stalking me. Like a wolf stalking his prey. He said he knew as soon as he saw me that I was the only woman for him."

"I'm not sure if that's romantic or creepy," JW commented quietly.

"I felt the same way," she smiled. "But he was very persuasive. And stubborn."

"I get it from both parents then," he noted with a bit of a smile.

"Yes, you do," she agreed.

"What happened?"

"A week before I was due to return to the States," she said quietly. He felt grief creep into her voice. "He had to go to his family's estates in the southeastern part of France, not far from the coast. He promised to return before I left so we could settle our plans to be together. Then—" Her entire body trembled. "A cousin came to the apartment. He said Jean had been killed in a car accident the day before. That he'd been in such a hurry to get back to me he'd taken a turn too fast and—"

JW wrapped both arms around her and shuddered at the emotion that poured out of her. *Over thirty years. She's kept that inside her for so long.*

"Why haven't you ever told me that when I asked?" He was more curious than upset.

"You were just a boy," she whispered. He could feel her wiping at her tears. "And you haven't asked since you were about twelve."

"Did he know you were pregnant?"

"I didn't even know," she replied, shaking her head. "You know how your grandmother is. She didn't tell me about the facts of life, puberty, or anything else. And back then, it wasn't something you could easily find out about by reading or asking anyone. I was home a month getting sick nonstop and she dragged me to the doctor for an exam. I was pregnant." Her green eyes met his. "And I had something to live for again. I had you. The man I loved was still alive in you."

Now, tears filled his eyes.

"You still love him," he marveled. "That's why you refuse to let Grandmother or anyone else set you up with anyone."

"You look just like him," she told him. "Except for my eyes. The O'Grady eyes. Your face and hair, your body shape, the way you move. Even your attitude toward some things. Sometimes my heart aches even as I think of how proud he would be. He wanted children so much," her voice faded.

She lifted the slender gold chain from her neck. JW couldn't remember a time when she hadn't worn it. Or the ring he saw dangling from it.

"His cousin said this was one of the few things that survived the fire from the crash. Jean had meant for me to have it."

With a new understanding, JW carefully caught the ring in his fingers. To remove the chain from his mother's neck never occurred to him.

"The stones?" he whispered.

"Emerald for May and topaz for November. Our birth months," she explained.

November. My father was born in November. The gems were surrounded by tiny diamonds set on a gold ring. Turning it, he frowned at the etching.

"What's this?" He indicated.

"The wolf head from the family crest."

"Did you ever contact them after that? Do they know about me?" *The thought of his father's family rejecting him hurt deep even though he'd never thought about them before.*

"I wrote to the cousin when I knew I was pregnant and when you were born," she replied. "There was no response."

"So, it really has just been me and you against the world," he whispered, recalling the song she would sing to him. His eyes darted to the door where the rest of the Franklins could be heard talking, then back to his mother's face. "You never told any of them."

"Who could I tell who would understand?" She shrugged. "Mother decreed that I'd succumbed to Paris madness and had a one-night stand. Daddy didn't say anything, and my brothers went along with Mother without question. The only one who ever even asked me about any of it was Paddy."

Nodding as he thought about what she'd said, JW thought of Paddy O'Grady, a cousin on his grandfather's side of the family. Paddy ran the Shadows clubs with his son Liam. Both of them had been born with the O'Grady "gift," even more so than his mother and cousins.

"Paddy," he echoed, then frowned as he looked down at his mother. A mischievous glint was in her eyes. "No," he shook his head. "No."

A smile quirked her lips.

"Easy, sweetheart. Rein in your imagination. I'm on the board but I don't participate."

The implications of that hit him and he swallowed.

"Dear God," he managed.

"Hush," she chuckled. "Like I said, don't go there."

"Yeah," JW heaved in a breath. "Yeah. Holy shit."

"You think your grandmother's had a chance to calm down?" Zoey changed the subject.

"I doubt it," he drawled. "But she'll put on a good face."

"Of that, I have no doubt," agreed his mother. "Come on. We're still Franklins."

She turned to go to the door, but he caught her arm. Quietly she stopped, waiting for him to speak.

"Thank you, Mom. For everything. I never understood what you'd gone through. I know I still don't, but, thank you. I hope I never let you down."

"Oh, sweetheart," she whispered, framing his face with her hands. "You could never do that as long as you always do your best each moment."

"Promise," he vowed, kissing her forehead.

"Now, let's go deal with my mother," she gritted out.

"We can't stay here?" he muttered, even as they fell into step together.

"Nice try."

Chapter Three

"Do I have to go?" Ally half-whined to Diana.

She knew she sounded like a five-year-old and didn't care. The few encounters she'd had with "high society" people had soured her on all of them.

Her cousin-in-law chuckled from the bed as she breastfed her newborn son. Nearly a month premature, Matt numbered among the countless others born when the stress of 9/11 had brought about early labor. Having gone to the office to get all his people clear, David had met up with friends to try to get home and arrived just thirty minutes before his son's birth.

"I know," the new mother sighed. "It seems a bit odd after this week, doesn't it? But some things never seem to affect people in a certain world."

"I'm not sure I like this world," Ally stated.

"Neither do I," agreed David as he leaned against the doorframe. "But it's only for a couple hours, Ally. I promise. And it's just a small group."

"Small as in how many?" she frowned. "In your social circle *small* is a relative term."

"I don't know," he admitted, then extended his hand. "Come on. We're not going into the lions' den."

"I'd rather face the lions," she told him, standing from where she'd been sitting on the bed. Halfway to the door, she glanced at Diana. "I'll trade you places."

That had the woman laughing.

"Nice try. The Franklins are nice people, Ally. They helped us deal with my family."

"I know," said Ally, joining her cousin at the door. "I'm just not good with crowds and I don't know any of your friends."

"That's why you're going to a *small* party first," David told her.

"If you say so," she sighed, rolling her eyes and making Diana laugh again.

In David's little sports car, Ally fastened her seat belt. "Okay, run through the family again."

Trying to remember the names and where they fit in, Ally braced herself when they drove through the open iron gates and around the circle drive. A jacketed valet opened her door and, accepting his assistance out, Ally waited on the flagstones for David to give the keys to another valet before joining her.

"Small parties have car valets?" she muttered.

"The Franklins do," he replied, leading her up the broad front steps to the open double doors.

"David, thank heavens," a deep voice greeted them as they entered the marble-floored foyer. "I was wondering if you'd come."

"Bron, how are you? This is my cousin, Ally. Careful, Ally," David whispered and winked. "Bron just passed his bar exam and is an actual, real-life lawyer now."

"So, you keep David out of trouble," Ally quipped, shaking the man's hand.

"I'm a lawyer, not a miracle worker," he replied with a grin. "Besides, that's Diana's job now. Thank God."

"And she does an amazing job of it," Ally agreed.

The light in Bron's brown eyes dimmed slightly as he became serious.

"JW's home," he said quietly.

Her cousin stiffened noticeably and inhaled sharply. "For how long?"

"Just until tomorrow."

"Shit," David breathed, closing his eyes briefly. "Where is he?"

"In the library with Grant and Nick. Aunt Zoey and Grandmother had it out earlier."

"About what?"

"Would you like me to leave?" Ally offered, ready to give them privacy but not having a clue as to where to go.

Shaking his head, Bron smiled at her.

"No need. I was just warning David. I have no doubt Grandmother will try to get him on her side."

"About what?" David frowned. "I'm hardly going to take sides in a family argument."

"Good luck with that," muttered Bron.

"Hello, David," a slender blonde woman greeted him as she joined them.

"Evening, Gisele," David greeted her with an air kiss. "My cousin, Ally. Bron's cousin Gisele."

"The center of calm," Gisele smiled warmly. "I need to stay with you." Linking arms, she eased her away from the men. "I'll take care of her, David."

"I've no doubt of that," he replied with a nod.

"What was all that about?" Ally whispered as Gisele guided her toward the front room.

"What was what about?" the blonde asked, waving to someone across the room.

"I don't mean to pry, but David seemed to tense up when Bron said JW was home. And something about Aunt Zoey and Grandmother."

"JW's the oldest Franklin cousin," Gisele explained. "He's a soldier in the Army. I guess Bron told David about the blow-up between Grandmother and Aunt Zoey," Gisele surmised. "Drink?" she offered, gesturing at the nearby bar.

"Water, please," Ally requested with a smile at the bartender. "I'm still on some meds after the accident."

"Bron told me about what you've been through," the younger woman replied, sympathy in her eyes. "I'm so sorry."

"Thank you," Ally managed. "Now, tell me who is here. David said it was small, but I got the feeling your grandmother has her own definition of *small*."

Giselle chuckled.

"Oh, she does. Stick with me. We'll get through it together."

***

"JW."

Turning at the familiar voice, JW smiled slightly at David's expression.

"Stop acting as if I'm dead or going to be," he muttered, shaking the man's hand. "Mom's not, so no one else is allowed to."

"Did you clue Grandmother in on that?" Nick muttered.

The Franklin cousins rolled their eyes in unison. After the argument with her daughter, Henrietta had adopted an air of impending doom. Through the open library doors, JW glimpsed Gisele going into the parlor with a small chestnut-haired woman. David followed his eyes.

"That's my cousin, Ally," he told him. "Gisele was kind enough to take care of her."

"Ally doesn't like parties?" Grant asked with a bit of surprise and condescending air.

"I'm not sure she's comfortable yet with *Long Island* parties," David answered. "Well, Long Island people, actually. This is her first party."

"And Grandmother is on the warpath," Nick grimaced. "Ouch. She'll never want to leave the house again."

"Nick," Grant muttered with a warning glance.

Wondering at the tingling he felt in his mind, JW watched the women disappear.

Staying mostly in the library and admitting to himself that he was trying to avoid his grandmother, JW kept an eye on those in the wide foyer. After an hour of sipping the same whisky, he saw Gisele talking to Nick near the stairs. Easing himself toward the door, he caught sight of Ally going out the parlor doors to the yard. Without hesitation, ignoring the smile on Gisele's face, he strode past them to catch up with Ally.

As the noise faded, Ally rounded a hedge and took a deep breath to relax, pressing her fingers to her temples.

"Breathe, breathe, breathe," she chanted.

"Does that work?" a deep voice asked behind her.

Gasping, she whirled and saw the oldest Franklin cousin. He had the same green eyes as his mother but, unlike the varying blonde shades of the other Franklins, his hair was dark. And cut short. *The soldier. About to go to war.*

"What really works is people sneaking up on me and scaring the life out of me so it doesn't matter if I have a pounding headache," she grumbled, a hand over her heart. "I'm dead so the headache doesn't matter."

"Sorry," he replied with a smile, taking her other hand and guiding her over to a bench. Easing her onto it, he sat next to her. "I wasn't trying to be quiet."

Catching her breath, she looked at him, finally smiling.

"It probably comes naturally to you by now. You're the soldier, aren't you?"

"Is that what they're calling me in there?"

He doesn't feel like he fits into his family. I know that feeling.

His eyes darted toward the rectangle panes of light coming from the mansion. Ally thought she caught some resentfulness in his gaze. And a bit of longing.

"I don't listen to gossip," she answered primly. "Giselle pointed you out a little while ago and said you were a soldier home on leave until tomorrow." Her voice dropped. "She said you wouldn't tell them where you were going."

"Because I don't know," JW answered.

"And if you did know, you wouldn't anyway," she smiled, exhaling as she tipped her head. "My grandpa and Uncle Jack were in the Army. They were always fussing about operational security and how politicians didn't have a clue about the concept."

Nodding, he chuckled slightly.

"When the final history of the world is written, they'll probably say more wars were lost by political loose lips than the soldiers fighting them."

"That's the truth," agreed Ally. The haunted expressions in their eyes came to mind and she put a hand on his well-muscled forearm. Startled, he looked down at her. "You will be careful, won't you? Please?"

For a long moment, he didn't speak. He just stared at her. Ally felt as if he could see through to her soul. His hand came up. First his fingertips brushed her cheek, then he cupped her jaw, his thumb moving back and forth over her lips.

"Give me a reason, Ally," he murmured, lowering his head. "Give me a reason to be careful."

"Like wha—"

His mouth came down over hers. Ally had been kissed before. She'd made out in the back of pick-up trucks after football games at home, but nothing had prepared her for the feel of his lips. His arms slid around her, pulling her off the bench and onto his lap. One hand held the back of her head, bracing it against the onslaught of his mouth. His tongue swept past her lips and tangled with hers, tugging and teasing. Moaning, Ally twisted toward him, pressing closer to his solid chest. Her hands moved along his arms, broad shoulders, and caught the back of *his* head.

It was like holding a bonfire. Every part of him heated up even as every part of him could only focus on the woman he held. JW was hard-pressed to maintain some control, to not pick her up and carry her behind some bushes to peel the column of silk covering her curves and— No, he didn't want to worry about the noise she would make. He wanted to hear her as he touched her. Suddenly, all he wanted was to hear her little whimpers and cries as he nibbled on her neck and thighs, her moans as he suckled on her breasts, her pleading pants as he tongued her pussy. Most of all, he needed her begging for permission to come. His cock sprang to attention, ready to go. *It's been so damn long.*

One hand covered a breast, fingers fondling, and he thought he'd come just from touching the soft mound. Ally arched slightly as if offering herself to him. And he was ready to dive into to her and take every velvety inch of her creamy skin.

"I saw him come this way," Bron's voice came through the shadows. "Think he's avoiding the party?"

Freezing, JW clutched the woman in his arms against his chest. *Damn it. I don't want them seeing us. This is just us. Just me and Ally.*

"Bron, he kinda has other things on his mind," Nick's voice responded from the other side of the hedge. JW realized how much his cousin had matured since the Fourth of July celebration. *No, just this week.* "And those things are a helluva lot more important than some damned party."

"You've changed your tune," Bron commented. "Before the school term started, you were all about finding out how the rest of us had sneaked out of the dorms with a bottle and—"

"Knock it off, Bron," snarled the younger cousin. "I felt thousands of people dying just a few days ago. Hundreds in pain. I felt their fear. I could feel . . ." his breath caught. "God, how did Gisele manage? Or Aunt Zoey? They were closer. So much closer," he whispered. "I need to talk to JW. I just know he felt something."

JW felt Ally shift on his lap and looked down at her astonished expression. He shook his head and she nodded, pressing her face to his shoulder.

Bron sighed audibly.

"You know, if you keep acting like this, Grandmother will do something drastic and you won't like it."

Nick snorted.

"Bron, there's nothing she could do that would be worse than what I felt on Tuesday. Trust me." He sighed. "Let's go inside. We can tell her he's not out here."

"She didn't send us looking for him," Bron pointed out. "Heather did."

"Man, for someone who just passed the bar exam with one of the highest scores, you are sure clueless when it comes to your own grandmother," Nick sneered. "Come on."

"You want a drink? I could sneak you one."

"No, I think I had enough Tuesday."

Listening to his cousins, JW cradled Ally, absently stroking her hair. As their voices and footsteps faded, he sighed.

"What was that about?" she whispered. "Or is that family stuff?"

"Definitely family stuff," he murmured. "Stuff my grandmother would rather pretend doesn't exist."

"JW," she breathed.

"Sh, Ally," he shook his head, knowing he had to end things before they even got started. "Don't say a word. Let me kiss you one more time. A soldier's farewell kiss from a lovely woman. Something to remind him what he's fighting for before he goes into the fire of combat."

Her lips, puffy from his first kiss, parted. He could see more words lurking in the shadows of her eyes and kissed her before she could say them.

He had seen it as Nick had talked about what he'd felt on the eleventh. His mother might have and pretended she hadn't, but he had just then. The image of an explosion. His body flying through the air and landing against the rocks, eyes closed as blood trickled down his face.

Desperate to feel alive before he died, he ravished Ally's mouth, his arms clutching her to him, letting her warmth fill him one more time. Only when they were both panting did he lift his head. Her eyes were closed as her head lolled against his shoulder. With a tenderness he'd only ever shown his mother, he brushed a tendril of hair from her temple, kissed her forehead and lifted her from his lap, easing her onto the bench. As she tried to catch her breath, he left her alone.

Warm, warmer, she was burning. Oh, no one had ever told her a kiss could make her feel so alive! Held by his strength, Ally felt safe. Safe and wanted. Panting on the bench, she rested her palm on the stone and leaned forward slightly, hoping the dizziness would fade. Then she realized he wasn't sitting beside her and lifted her head, certain he would be standing in the small secluded grove. Unable to believe it, she wrapped her arms around her stomach, eyes searching the shadows. Feeling utterly bereft, she slowly got up and went to find David.

****

Hearing the baby's fussing, Ally smiled slightly. He didn't fuss for long. Diana was quick to respond to her son. Being around baby Matt had made Ally think of the future again. It hurt, but she knew her family would have wanted her to keep going. And she was working on it. She really was. *Physical therapy first. Let's get the legs working again properly, shall we?* Ally chuckled as she swung those same legs over the edge of the mattress. She was picking up some of Diana's way of speaking. That delighted her cousin-in-law, while making David roll his eyes. Showered and dressed, she left her room and headed slowly down the hall to the staircase.

She still marveled at the size of the Brown mansion. When David had told her it was actually one of the smaller of the old cottages, she hadn't believed him until they'd shown her around a week after she'd moved in with them. The Brown house had "only" ten family bedrooms, including the four on the nursery level. Most of the larger mansions had at least a dozen.

David was in the southern facing sunroom they usually breakfasted.

"He woke you up again?" he greeted her.

"Your son has a very strong set of lungs," she chuckled, going to the sideboard to get coffee. "Especially at breakfast time."

"Or whenever else he wants his mother's attention," David murmured. At Ally's puzzled glance, David waved a hand. "Don't worry about that."

"Um, no, nice try," Ally told him, sitting down at the small round table. "Is everything okay with you and Diana?"

"Absolutely," he assured her with a smile. "I'm just hoping that one of these days, rather nights, he sleeps for more than three hours at a time so she can."

"Is Diana okay? Health wise?"

Ally had heard about new mothers having postpartum depression and reminded herself to keep an eye out for it. *David probably won't think of that.* And he confirmed that with his next words.

"She's simply exhausted. I can't tell you how glad I am that you're here." He caught himself. "Not how or why you're here, but—"

"It's okay," she whispered. "I know what you mean."

He held her gaze for a long moment then nodded.

"She trusts you with Matt, as do I. That means she's able to get some rest when he's awake. I can't tell you what that means to me."

Ally smiled. Because of what the pair had gone through with their families, there weren't many they trusted with their precious baby.

"So, what's the plan for today?" she asked.

"Board meeting at ten," he replied with a grin. "You ready?"

Ally groaned and sent him a pleading glance. "Do I have to?"

"Yup," he nodded, digging his fork into his omelet. "I think if we work things right, we can get the last of the oldsters out in the next couple weeks. Their probable replacements aren't much better, but the feedback I've received from the stockholders is that they feel more confident the company was going forward with the leadership changes the past eleven months. Especially," he waved the fork at her and winked, "since the Brown family is showing signs of interest in the future."

Rolling her eyes, she laughed.

"Well, whatever I can do to help the cause then."

"Atta, girl," he nodded. "Better eat up though. Dealing with those assholes requires all the energy you can muster."

"Is this you pumping me up?" she wondered, going to the sideboard and getting a plate. She scooped up eggs and picked out two link sausages. "Because you're terrible at it."

"Sorry," he replied. "I'm working on that part of life. You and Diana have been getting pretty good at softening the edges, but every now and then . . ." David sighed and shook his head as she sat down. "I should warn you, Ally. Business gets vicious in ways the papers never report because no one in the meetings will ever admit to what really happened. Most of them are still trying to figure out if you're a legitimate Brown."

"I've seen some of that in the papers," she said. "I still don't understand how Grandfather was able to erase a son so completely."

"Same way the Kennedys basically erased a daughter," shrugged David.

"They just sent her away and stopped talking about her," Ally murmured, still amazed at that. "Grandfather destroyed documents and . . ." She frowned. "No one ever wondered how he was a 'fourth,' but didn't name his supposed only son the 'fifth'?"

"Yeah, that should have been a big clue," drawled David. "I finally figured out the timing though," he continued quietly. "Grandmother killed herself three weeks after your father died in the storm. And that's about the same time my father started drinking so heavily."

"What about Grandfather's reaction?" Ally wondered. "Surely the death of his oldest son did something to him?"

"Not that I can tell," David answered with a shake of his head. "He was a cold-hearted bastard."

"And your mother? Wasn't she the one my father refused to marry?" Ally frowned trying to recall the ins and outs. David and Diana had explained it to her in Maine and she'd resolutely put it out of her mind. Healing had taken all her energies.

"She'd overdosed on sleeping pills years before," he said quietly, then met her eyes. "The day after the law firm told Grandfather about you being born."

Ally stared at him, feeling as if someone had punched her in the gut.

"Oh, my God," she breathed.

"Yeah," he muttered, stabbing a sausage. "The family history is fucked up and we have to pick up the pieces."

"How?" she gasped. "My God, David, you just told me that—"

"Hey, neither of us had anything to do with what our fathers or their parents did," he said sternly, reaching out and covering her hand. "You at least had some semblance of a loving family life, right?"

"Yeah," she whispered, nodding, still in shock as she tried to process what he'd told her.

"That's more than Diana or I had, so we're counting on you to teach us. Tell us what your parents did and such. I, at least, had friends who were like brothers in school. She has a tyrant for a father whose belief system regarding families is from . . ." David shook his head. "God, I don't know what century he's from. But he's not going to be around our kids. I can guarantee that. We'll create our own family and future, Ally. None of us are alone anymore."

"I know, but I don't fit in here," she whispered. "You grew up around all this money. For heaven's sake, Diana's got a title. Me? I'm from a little fishing village in Maine."

"Yes, but you're also a Brown. Don't forget that. You are part of the family. Not just the company."

"I won't," she replied. Deep inside though, she felt very uncertain about where she belonged.

Chapter 4
Christmas Eve, 2001

The shadows lengthened and the light foot traffic on the paths dwindled. Sunset came early in the Afghan mountains. Blending in with the brush and rocks around them, two men focused on the group across the valley.

"That's the Taliban leader for this province," breathed the spotter. "He's turning . . . now."

Peering through the scope, JW squeezed the trigger and the brief *thhhhppp* of the bullet leaving the chamber was softer than a whisper.

"Bingo," murmured the prone man lying next to the sniper. "One dead Taliban."

"The group he was with looks a little surprised," JW replied, lining up his next target. "See any other activity?"

There was a pause and he knew Parker was sweeping the valley with his high-powered binoculars. "Nothing," came the whisper. "Second bogey is moving out of range though."

"I see him." JW had anticipated their target's reaction and was waiting. He calmly pulled the trigger again, grateful that the rifle's silencer protected the location of their position.

"Two dead bad guys," his partner reported to their superiors over the radio. "We're getting out before—"

"They're looking for snipers," JW cut in, packing up his rifle. "Let's get out before things get hot, Parker."

Parker carefully inched away from their position and moved along their exit route. JW slipped in quickly behind him. Neither man made a noise and blended seamlessly into their surroundings. As they worked their way down the rocky crag, they paused often to listen for any sounds of pursuit.

Four long hours later, making their way slowly back to HQ, a snap in the brush brought them to a halt. In one movement, both were back-to-back, crouching with their weapons aimed at the rocks around them. Mentally, JW cursed himself. Just because they were within a mile or two of base was no reason to get sloppy or complacent.

"I didn't know there were wolves in Afghanistan," a clipped Boston accent came from JW's right.

"Friend," murmured JW to Parker, lowering his weapon and standing. Parker followed suit.

Captain Ben Hancock emerged from behind a large rock. Two steps behind him stood a rangy sergeant who studied them with obvious suspicion. Definitely a friend. The Franklin and Hancock families had known each other since before the Revolution. Ben and Grant had been two years behind JW at the elite prep school, with Brian Hancock between their years and more Hancocks and Franklins younger. Ten more men appeared around the new arrivals.

"I didn't know there were ships in the mountains," JW replied with a rare smile, referring to the shipping industry that had made the Hancock fortune. "What the hell are you doing here?"

"Just heading back from patrol. Quincy heard you coming." Gesturing to the sergeant behind him whose brown eyes were still narrowed in suspicion, Hancock strode forward and embraced his friend. "Gotta make sure you make it back safely to give Grant a hand."

"Like hell," JW snorted.

JW wasn't sure what he could do possibly do for the family company. All he knew was the military. Of course, he could always take down those pesky business competitors . . . the hard and permanent way. He'd mentioned it to Grant as his cousin drove him to the small airport for the family plane to return him to his duty station. His cousin had laughed shortly and said not to tempt him.

"Let's get you back to HQ," Ben urged before JW could say more.

"What's happened?" JW could see the tension in the younger man's eyes.

"How long have you been out of touch?" Ben asked.

"We headed out with our second list of targets 15 November," he replied, praying there hadn't been another attack. "We know about the anthrax attacks. What else has happened?"

"Some idiot tried to blow up a Paris to Miami flight three days ago," Ben informed him. "The explosives were in his shoes."

"Tried?" Parker frowned. "He wasn't successful?"

"Passengers stopped him," Hancock grinned as they walked down the rocky path toward base. Hancock's men fell into position around them. JW approved of their protectiveness around their leader. And not just because he liked Ben or that he was an officer. If the Taliban knew who Ben was, they'd realize what kind of prize was under their noses. "United 93's heroes may have changed the course of history in many ways."

"Thank God for them," JW sighed, then frowned at the captain. "Don't tell me Grant asked you to drag me back to New York City."

"Hell, no!" Ben laughed. "And if he tried, I'd just laugh in his face. There's as much chance of you working for him as there is of me working for my cousin. And, yeah, Brian brought it up before I left. I told him there was more important work to do here."

"I hear you on that. What other news is there?"

By the time they'd reached the base's fenced perimeter, Ben had brought them up to speed. The MPs at the main gate eyed JW and Parker suspiciously as they were dressed as natives and had no identification on them. The pair glanced at each other. *One of the downsides of going deep undercover.* Parker rolled his eyes and tried again.

"Corporal, we were here as the camp was being set up. I could draw you a map to our tent. Would you like it in feet, meters, or steps you need to take?"

Both of the guards scowled at Parker's impatient tone.

"Corporal, these men are Americans," Ben vouched for them. "If you won't take my word for it—"

"Yes, sir," one soldier replied, stepping aside to let them through.

"Thanks," JW muttered.

"No problem," Ben replied, turning to his soldiers. "Men, go get some chow and shut eye. I'll report in and see where we go next."

Nodding, his company headed toward their tents. JW nodded at Parker, who headed to their tent with both of their packs. JW continued with Ben to the only wooden structure in the encampment.

"No sign of bin Laden?" JW wondered hopefully, although he knew Ben would have mentioned that first.

"Not yet. Odds are the asshole slipped over into Pakistan. We'll get him though. It may take a few years, but in this," Ben paused and looked over at him, "we will not waver in locating and killing the son of a bitch responsible for so many deaths."

"And God bless the man who pulls the trigger," JW murmured with conviction.

"I'll drink to that," Ben agreed with a sigh. "We all want vengeance; however, the politicians and media want to pretty it up by calling it justice."

"Hooah." JW pushed the door of the colonel's HQ open and they went to report.

A couple hours later, bathed and in clean uniforms, leaving the beards in place for their next mission, JW and Parker picked up their mail and went in search of food. Plates piled high, they found two empty spaces across from each other. The food was half gone before they slowed down and opened their mail.

"Your mom still writing every other day?" Parker asked with a smile.

Zoey's letters, especially her commentary about New York City society, had been about the only highlight during their previous deployments. JW nodded, sorting them out to put the oldest on top. He'd tried it the other way once and had gone three letters into the pile before learning that lesson. It was hard enough keeping up with his mother's mind when he was with her. There was no point in trying to complicate things from halfway around the world. She'd thought that amusing and helped him out by writing the mailing date in the lower left corner of each envelope.

They refilled their iced tea and rested forearms on the table as they read, exchanging commentary on what members of their families had done. On the second one, JW froze. He hadn't read that right. He couldn't have. Draining half his tea, he took a deep breath and tried to focus.

. . . I don't know if you met David Brown's newfound cousin, Ally. Or Alessandra as Mother insists on calling her. I'm not sure how, but Kevin MacLauren convinced her to elope with him to Vegas. You can imagine David's reaction. He's absolutely furious and beside himself about it. Gisele was stunned and quite upset—

It was still there in his mother's neat handwriting. He put the letter down, feeling light-headed. Impossible. How could she do that after that kiss? To turn around and be with MacLauren? He glanced at the date—20 October. Damn, he'd just missed getting this before they'd headed out. *Probably a good thing.*

"Yo, you okay?" Parker wondered. "The family all right?"

"Mm?" JW glanced up at him and blinked. "Yeah, everyone's okay."

"Has Nick stolen any more brandy?"

"Not yet," JW drawled. *Gisele was upset? I'm on the other side of the planet and I can't fucking believe it.*

Carefully folding the letter along the original folds, he returned it to the envelope and stared at the stack he still had to read. He didn't want to read about her marital bliss. *Please. She's married to MacLauren. Whatever bliss there might be in marriage, I know damn well she won't have with him.*

The man was the same age as Grant and Ben, and the most arrogant bullying coward JW had ever come across. The autumn after he'd joined the Army, Ben's cousin Brian had written to him about how Kevin and a group of his sycophant bullies had targeted scholarship student Tony Henderson and nearly beaten him to death. Over the years, MacLauren's violence had extended to women. There was never any direct link between Kevin and the women, of course. Their word against his and he always had friends giving him solid alibis. *And now he's married to Ally. What the fuck? Didn't David warn her about him?* But JW knew how charming Kevin could be, and Ally wouldn't have been able to withstand his seduction. *But why would he go after Ally?*

Gathering his courage, as if he was about to face down a thousand Taliban, JW reached for the next letter. Thankfully, his mother didn't mention Ally and her new husband in any of them.

Three days later, having written his usual bland one-page letter to his mother, mostly to reassure her he was still alive, he and Parker headed out again. JW felt an emptiness in his soul that hadn't been there before. *One kiss. It was one damned kiss. We were both free agents. She had every right to be with whomever she wanted. Yeah, but why the hell did it have to be that asshole?*

Returning to base two weeks later, having easily found and eliminated their targets, JW and Parker followed the same routine: report in, shower, clean their weapons, pick up mail, and get chow. His eyes lit up at the boot-size box with his cousin's handwriting.

"Who's that from?" Parker asked hopefully.

"Heather wrote the address," JW smiled. "God knows what is inside. And we were out so long it'll be stale."

"And your point?" Parker demanded, eyes on the box.

Their gazes clashed and both chuckled. The chow tent was mostly empty and, after loading up their trays, they spread out at a table. Sorting the letters first, JW grinned when Parker's eyes kept going to the box.

"Shit, you're worse than a begging dog," he muttered, rolling his eyes and reaching for the box.

"Woof, woof. Hurry up. You're a master at torturing me."

Cutting the tape, JW flipped the flaps out of the way and chuckled.

"They know you."

Reaching in, he took out the brown lunch bag labeled "Parker" and tossed it to him.

"Sweet," his partner crooned. "My own stash of goodies."

"What's in there?" JW asked as Parker peered inside.

"Why? I'm not sharing with you," Parker retorted.

"Asshole."

JW flipped him off as he laughed.

"Yeah, yeah, read the first letter and give me the next installment of the Long Island bubble people."

Chuckling, JW finished his meat, or what was being classified as meat, and opened the first letter. Parker was contentedly working on his plate, the paper bag on his lap.

Reading aloud snippets of how Nick had done in basketball or Heather had aced a series of exams, JW scanned ahead and stopped talking. *I mentioned in a letter last month how Ally Brown had eloped with Kevin MacLauren. He had it annulled after only six weeks of marriage, and is now publicly discussing how bad she was in the bedroom. During the party three nights ago, it took Grant, Bron, a couple visiting Hancocks, and several others to drag David out of the room before he could attack Kevin. Poor Ally was there and no one has seen her since. I can't blame her at all, although I don't believe a word Kevin is saying about her. I don't want to shock the tender ears of my sweet, innocent child, but Kevin MacLauren is an asshole and I hope he rots in the depths of hell.*

"Wow," he murmured.

Mom is thoroughly pissed at Kevin. I wonder if she knows any witch's spells or something to turn him into a rock or something.

Not yet. If she could, she'd have written that she'd done it and then talked about the weather without skipping a beat.

"What's up?" Parker's question brought JW out of the letter from home.

"My mother just called someone an asshole," JW told him.

"Your mother? Your sweet mother? The one who gets along with just about everyone on the planet?" Parker stared at him in doubt. "Damn. Asshole must be one bad dude. Do we head home and put him six feet under?"

"Don't tempt me, Parker. Don't tempt me," JW replied, trying to fight the urge to do just that.

****

As April showers lashed at the windows, Ally glared at her therapist.

"No," she stated firmly. "I refuse to accept that."

The sixty-something man sighed as he removed his steel-rimmed glasses and cleaned the lenses. Frustrated, Ally ground her molars and waited for him to respond. Putting the glasses back on, he gave her a condescending look.

"And that is the root of your problem, Ally. You refuse to accept responsibility for your actions."

"My actions? What actions? I didn't *do* anything. I never had a chance! My ex filed for the annulment because my cousin wouldn't do business with him," she pounded her fists against her thighs in frustration. "How is that my responsibility? I don't have anything to do with either of their businesses."

"Your ex-husband clearly thought you had more influence on your cousin. In that regard, you deceived him," came the pompous statement.

Dumbfounded, Ally felt her jaw go slack.

"I deceived him? Everyone knows my cousin and I were strangers until last June. David and Diana didn't know about me until . . ."

Choking back the sob that, if it came up, would open the dam of emotions she constantly fought to control, Ally turned away.

"Until the car accident that killed your mother, her father, and her brother," the therapist stated in the calm, oh-so-reasonable voice that drove her up a wall. "Your ex-husband had every reason—"

"To blame me for every problem in his life?" Ally questioned, not caring about being rude. "For traffic? For bad weather? For how the stocks reacted? If he spilled coffee on himself? For not responding to him sexually?"

"Well, that last, yes," the man replied. "Certainly."

"Well, I'm sorry," she responded sarcastically, unable to hold it back any longer. "But it takes more than wham, bam, thank you ma'am to get me going in bed."

"So, you think he should have been more romantic? Put a little more effort into things?" he said in a milder tone.

Ally blushed slightly at the turn in the conversation, but nodded even as she fought back the memory. *Strong arms wrapping around her, lean muscles against her soft body a shield against the world. A hand at the back of her head and then a kiss to rock her world.*

"Yes, I think he should have. He expected me to be ready anytime he wanted to have sex, and if I wasn't, it was my fault." She paced around the room, growing angrier with every step. "It wasn't my fault," she muttered. "I don't make the final decisions. Kevin knew that. He had no right to blame me for everything that went wrong in his life."

"Are you angry, Ally?"

"No, I'm not angry. Dammit," she replied, shooting a glare at him across the room. "I'm pissed."

Actually, I'm frustrated because the man I want is on the other side of the planet and there's not a damn thing I can do about any of it.

"Well, it's about damned time," Dr. Jones exulted.

"What?" She stared at him, as he grinned smugly at her. "You tricked me."

"Ally, for too long now, you've simply accepted what life threw at you. You'd take it and do nothing." He smiled and leaned back in his chair, putting his steno pad and pen on the table next to him. "Finally, you're angry. No, I like your word better. *Pissed.* Now," he jabbed a finger at her, "what are you going to do about it?"

Ally blinked and collapsed on the couch.

"I haven't the slightest idea," she admitted.

"Well, it's still a start," he told her. He bent his right leg so the ankle rested on his left knee and steepled his fingers as his elbows rested on the shin. "We've got the mental part of your recovery moving, and your physical therapy is completed?" He paused until she nodded in agreement. "So, it looks like the only thing you need to work on is the sexual part. Because of what your ex did."

Ally felt the heat of another blush cover her face. *Damn attacks. If we'd had more time . . . no, no wishful thinking. What ifs will only drive me crazy.*

"I didn't think that was your line of work," she frowned, wondering how far they would take that line of therapy. *Dr. Jones isn't suggesting that we –*

He laughed.

"No, it's not by any stretch of the imagination."

Ally shook her head.

"I don't think I need sex therapy. I'm not planning on having it anymore, so it doesn't matter."

"Ally—"

A glare shut him up so fast she could hear his teeth snap together.

"I've had more than enough to last me a lifetime." *I'm absolutely not discussing sex with anyone. Enough.*

He sighed.

"I've heard rumors about Kevin MacLauren."

"Oh, I'm sure," she muttered. "Everyone's heard rumors, but no one has done a damn thing to find out the truth. No one believes any woman who says a damned thing against him." She squeezed her eyes shut. *David just shook his head, saying he warned me about him. Like I deserved to be treated—* Ally forced the sob back down her throat. "So, he continues ruining lives. What will it take for someone to stop him?"

"There is a difference. Some couples, some women, like sex the way Kevin does."

"Bullshit," Ally snorted. "You don't know what you're talking about."

"So, you need to explore that side of life. In a safe environment," he said with an almost clinical detachment.

Opening her mouth to comment, Ally blinked as she ran his words through her mind. *What did he say? Safe environment? To explore sex?* She stared across the room at him. He hesitated, then shrugged as if making an internal decision.

"Tell David and Diana what I said. They'll know what to suggest."

"David and Diana?" She frowned. "Why would my cousin and his wife…"

"Trust me, Ally," he said quietly. "They'll know." There was a tap at the door. "Ah, excellent timing. I think we've made some real progress today."

"You're not going to tell me, are you?"

He winked at her. "Like you said, that's not my line of work."

Her mind elsewhere as she went through the revolving front door. Ally stumbled on the sidewalk, made slippery by the spring rain, and slid into the waiting car with all the grace of a three-legged cat. Her ankle twisted and she felt pain shoot up her leg. The chauffer hesitated and looked in before he shut the door.

"Are you all right, Miss Brown?"

Tears filled her eyes as she shook her head, lightly touching her ankle.

"I'll head straight home unless there's somewhere else you'd like to go?"

"No, nowhere else," she whispered. "Just home, please, Robinson."

"Very well, Miss."

The door clicked shut softly and Ally closed her eyes, feeling tears track wetly down her cheeks. Nowhere to go. Except a home that wasn't hers.

In late October, as she'd finally started to adjust, she'd been swept off her feet by Kevin MacLauren. David had warned her to be careful, but she'd been caught up in the fairy tale being spun, especially when Kevin had suggested they fly to Vegas in his private jet to elope just three weeks after meeting. When David refused to consider her husband's business deal, she'd literally been tossed out of the apartment after Kevin had— She moaned helplessly at that memory.

In public at every holiday gathering, he'd talked about her inability to respond, calling her frigid. Unable to bear that humiliation on top of everything else, Ally had drunk herself into a stupor and shut herself off completely a couple weeks.

Worried and exasperated, David had finally insisted she start seeing a therapist in January. Now, despite everything, Ally felt like she was still running in place. All she wanted was security. Secure surroundings. A secure relationship. David and Diana cared about her, and they accepted her simply because she was *family*. But they didn't *know* her.

Then again, given her history, Ally didn't know herself.

As the car picked up speed, Ally took a deep breath and exhaled, shaking away painful memories. David wanted her to give the therapist an honest effort. She had, she really had, but she still felt absolutely lost.

During predinner drinks, she told them about that afternoon's session.

"He tricked you into getting pissed? Into losing your temper?" Diana stared at her. "Damn, I would've tried that if I'd thought it was possible. You are seriously the most calm person I've ever known."

Ally grinned and raised her wine glass in response.

"What did he mean about working on the sexual part? In a safe environment? And asking the two of you about it?" wondered Ally.

Diana drew in a breath and shot a look at her husband.

"That one is yours, darling."

"Okay," David murmured, sipping his scotch. "We've tried doing what society tells us to do to fix things. Now, how about we try something a bit more drastic, a bit . . . outside the box?"

Stunned, Ally stared at him.

"Why didn't you bring this up before?"

"Because it's not something most people would understand," he paused and cleared his throat nervously. "I wanted to give you a chance to go the traditional route first. To be sure."

Ally thought she'd truly go insane as he verbally danced about.

"Spit it out, David."

The silence drew out and she studied his face. He really was hesitant about mentioning it to her. What on earth could he be considering that had her normally extremely confident, alpha male cousin feeling nervous? *Sex? No way could that make David uneasy. Unless it's having to talk about it to his publicly embarrassed cousin.*

"David, we've tried therapy, solo and in a group. I could probably stock a library with all the self-help books I have in my room. Tell me." Ally felt weary at the sidestepping.

"Hear me out before you react," he started. She nodded. "We've tried fixing the mental and physical side of this equation. The physical therapy's gone well, and it looks like you've made a good breakthrough on the mental. Tim's right. We need to do something a bit more drastic to get you over what Kevin did in the short time you were married." He frowned. "My reaction when you came home that day screwed you up more, didn't it?"

She nodded and he muttered an oath.

"I'm sorry for that," David told her. "I truly am."

Wrapping her arms around herself, Ally just nodded again.

"Legally there isn't anything that could be done," Diana sighed. "It's the most ridiculous law I've ever heard of."

"I could go beat him to a pulp," David offered. "Put him in the hospital for a while."

"I'm not sure that would reassure the board," Ally said with a patience she wasn't feeling.

Now he says something like that. Marital rape isn't recognized as a crime in New York, so there was nothing I could do that last day. Nothing any of us could do.

"Fuck the board," he replied ferociously. "Dammit, Ally. I feel like shit for reacting the way I did when you came home."

"We'll have to all stay aware and make sure he doesn't do it to anyone else," Diana stated firmly. "And find some other way to make him pay."

"Oh, that will be an absolute pleasure," David promised.

"So, what do we do?" Ally prompted. "What the doctor was talking about?"

"I have an idea about that," he ventured, glancing at his wife. "But I need to talk to a friend about it first."

"David, do you really intend to take Ally to the *Shadows*?" Diana's question seemed a mix of surprise and incredulity.

Ally's head swiveled toward Diana. She'd heard of the midtown night spot.

"Shadows? How would a nightclub help me?"

"It's not entirely a nightclub," replied Diana, frowning at her husband. "At least, not the part Tim was thinking and David is suggesting. David, are you serious?"

He sighed and nodded.

"I think it might be good for her."

"Why *didn't* you bring that up sooner?" Diana asked in frustration.

"We owed it to Ally to try the usual routes of therapy," David replied quietly. "No point in shocking her before she'd had some chance of recovery."

"Good point," his wife replied with a nod. Her brown eyes met her husband's. "But am I right in assuming that you want Liam O'Grady to take Ally into the Shadows? Under a contract?"

"Yes," he answered with a meaningful glance at his wife that Ally didn't understand.

"You sure that's a good idea?" Diana frowned. "That bastard did a number on her."

"Diana!" David gave her chiding glance for her language.

"All right," she conceded with an eyeroll. "Let's just call him a son-of-a-bitch then." She smiled and winked at Ally. "I dealt with his mother at a fundraiser, so I know that's the truth."

A giggle burst from Ally's lips. Her cousin smiled at her response.

"Haven't heard much of that lately."

She relaxed a bit and curled up in the chair.

"So, is Liam a sex therapist?"

"Not quite," he paused and glanced at his wife.

"Just tell her. She can handle it, David," Diana advised. "She's stronger than she realizes."

He nodded and looked at Ally.

"Liam runs a sex club. I think you should join it and sign a contract. Not too long, but enough to work through things. The usual contract is six months, including about six weeks of training."

Ally froze, not even sure if she was breathing.

"A . . . a what?" She shook her head to clear it. No such luck. "David, I'm no good at sex. Obviously, given—"

"I don't give a rat's ass what that asshole said." David stood, came up to her chair, put his hands on the armrests, and leaned over her. "He was wrong. About everything. Got it?"

She swallowed and nodded.

"What could Liam do when nothing else has worked?"

"It's not so much what he can *do*, but the opportunity he would give you." David backed away and, picking up his glass, went to the bar for a refill.

"To do what?" Ally's confusion must have been evident, even to them.

"Well, he would need you to complete a questionnaire to help determine what you are."

"What I *am?*" she blinked. "I don't follow you."

"To see if you're a submissive or a dominant. Your answers also will help pinpoint what you're most likely to respond to sexually," David seemed to hesitate over the last word

"That's the problem," she muttered. "I don't respond to anything."

Except on moonlit nights in September with a man who disappeared on me.

David mumbled a few obscenities under his breath as he returned to his seat.

"Enough of that or I'll put you over my knee and spank you myself."

"That would be too perverse even for you," his wife spoke up. She leaned forward and touched Ally's knee. "The Shadows trains members according to the results of the questionnaire. Submissives have very different roles than dominants within the club."

"The Shadows," Ally echoed.

"Everything that happens inside the Shadows is confidential," Diana continued. "You'd sign an agreement and you *never* refer to it in public, even with another member."

"Submissives and dominants," Ally echoed, rolling those words through her mind. "What are they specifically? How do I fit into this?"

"Ally, given your nature," Diana started with a smile. "You've got to be a submissive. You prefer the dominant to take control. He or she . . ."

"He," Ally said firmly. "I might not know much about sex and pleasure, but I know I prefer men."

"Fair enough. He would determine when and how you felt pleasure," Diana continued, with a smile at her husband.

"If I were a submissive, what could be done to me?"

Ally felt her curiosity rising. Again, the feel of JW's arms around her came to mind. Oh, she could just imagine him as a dominant in sex. *Whatever the hell that means.*

"You decide on the parameters of a scene," David told her. "As mild or extreme as you are comfortable with or excited by."

"Slow down and back up a bit. What's a scene?" she asked, waving her hands to get his attention.

"A scene begins when a Master chooses a submissive and continues for a specified and agreed amount of time," he explained. "Some subs have hard limits. Others quite a few soft limits. The Master agrees to follow those guides. A submissive chooses a safe word. If he or she says it during a scene, the Master must stop."

"I'm confused," she whispered, blinking and shaking her head. "Granted, I don't know much and only from rumors and such, but I thought the Master controlled everything. From what you said, the submissive does."

"The sub sets the boundaries," elaborated Diana. "Within those limits, the control is the Master's right up to or if a sub uses the safe word."

"And if the Master doesn't stop?" Ally wondered. She didn't know what to think about what they were telling her.

"Fortunately, that doesn't happen often. But when it does, the Master faces various penalties set by the board," David replied. "Liam O'Grady is president of the board of members. His family started the club a hundred and fifty some odd years ago. Liam is very proactive and protective about safeguarding submissives and slaves."

"It's just sex?" she frowned. "Sounds like an elaborate prostitution ring."

"No," he replied firmly. "The Shadows is a safe, anonymous place where people can explore and enjoy their sexuality. And it's not just about sex. Sometimes sex doesn't even happen. For some, it's about exerting control or giving it up. That's the freedom of it. And no one judges you. Unless, of course, you step out of line and harm someone."

"So, there can't be that many people who are part of it. Someone would have said something to expose it."

Ally was mystified that an organization like that could exist in today's society without detection. *And it had been founded that long ago? How could anything like that be kept secret?*

"No, because most members come from society and business. The resulting publicity would ruin you, your family, and your business," David said wryly.

Ally smirked and nodded.

"That certainly would keep a lot of people quiet. People have a hard time accepting sex as a normal topic of conversation." She met his gaze and grimaced. "Unless it puts someone without any power in a very bad light."

"Exactly," David confirmed. "And, remember, it's not all about sex. For a lot of people, it's about control, even if it's over one thing, one very important thing in a person's life." He sat down on the footstool in front of Ally's chair and gripped her hands. "And I think that is what you need. You've never had control over anything. Grandfather was a straitlaced Puritan who wanted your father to marry a woman he had picked out. Your father didn't follow his dictates, so you never knew any of our family. Then that damn drunk driver took those you did know. Same for your marriage; Kevin took advantage of you at your weakest moment."

"He thought that, with us being married, you would sign that contract for the South Pacific resort." Ally grimaced at the humiliating memory.

"In his dreams," David snorted. "You see what I mean, though? The Shadows would give you a chance to determine your limits, to become more comfortable with sex, around people, and with men, in particular."

Ally chewed on her bottom lip and looked at Diana for support.

"Nothing else is working, is it?"

"It doesn't look like it, dear," she agreed.

They were silent as she thought for several minutes. While quite startled by the suggestion at first, the more David and Diana had talked, the more appealing it sounded.

"You're both members?" Ally glanced from one to the other.

"I'm a Dom," David replied. "Diana is my sub, if you can believe it."

His wife grinned and stuck her tongue out at her husband. At the heated look David gave Diana and the way she blushed and ducked her head, Ally smiled then stared at the flickering flames.

"I can hear the wheels spinning in your head, Ally," David spoke after she'd been silent a few moments. "What are you thinking?"

"What about STD's? And birth control stuff?" she asked hesitantly, trying to feel her way through this totally out-of-the box idea.

"Everyone is checked before admittance and at regular intervals, depending on how often they're at the Shadows and have different partners. Condoms are used, depending on the parties involved. And for birth control for women—" David glanced at his wife.

"The women under contract get those arm implants. If they do get pregnant, since only abstinence is a hundred percent, then they are fully taken care of regardless of what they chose to do."

Ally nodded, considering that. She smiled sadly.

"We fought about that," she whispered. "Having children. I wanted to start a family, and he thought I was crazy." Tears filled her eyes. "I should have seen it coming after some of the things he said. He didn't consider me in the same 'class' as him. The Brown family is, of course," she continued with a grimace. "But my mother was a nobody and that makes me low class. He said he couldn't possibly consider having a child with someone like me."

"Oh, Ally," sympathized Diana. "He's such an asshole."

"I don't like most of the people in your 'upper level of society'," Ally told them bluntly. "So convinced they're superior. So damned arrogant. There are exceptions, of course. To a point." She shrugged. "Then again, I've always been a bit different than everyone. I've never quite fit in and I don't understand why."

"You fit in with us," David told her quietly but firmly.

"I appreciate that, David, but I have to find a way to live on my own terms." Ally chuckled. "Once I figure out what those are, of course."

Sipping her wine, she stared at the flames while David and Diana talked quietly.

What the hell did she have to lose by going to this sex club? If all it did was get her over her ex, then it would be worth it. She could start living again. Hell, she might even find a man she could trust the way Diana trusted David.

Finally, she lifted her head and smiled, feeling good about a course of action for the first time in months.

"David, I'd like to meet your friend Liam."

Chapter Five

His cousins gave him only Thursday night to recover from jetlag. Having been in bed when he arrived, Heather, Nora, and Penny burst into his room before heading to school.

"You're here!" Heather shouted, throwing open the door.

Awake at the sound of the doorknob turning, JW was already sitting up and reaching for the weapon that wasn't there. Totally ignorant of the fact that their oldest cousin would have shot them, the three teenagers rushed to the bed and hugged him, their babble both calming and unsettling him.

"Girls," Zoey called from the door. "If you don't leave in two minutes, you're late."

Groaning, Nora kissed JW's cheek.

"Grandfather insisted we all go to school today. It's not fair! It's your first day back and we couldn't stay up last night."

Catching his breath, JW hugged each of them, kissing their foreheads.

"I'll be here for ten days," he reminded them. "Now, get going before you end up in trouble. That would not be a good way to start my leave."

Penny stepped back first and he winked at her. With a shy smile, she started to leave first. Heather and Nora had other plans.

"If you talked to Grandfather . . ." Heather spoke up.

". . . then he might let us stay home," Nora continued.

"Yeah, uh, no," he denied, shaking his head. "Scoot."

Groaning, they obeyed and followed Penny out of the room. JW blinked a couple times to recover from the energy rush they provided and glanced at his mother.

"Did you get the name of the truck that just ran over me?" he wondered.

Laughing, she shook her head.

"You get enough sleep?" she asked, walking to the foot of the bed.

"Mom, I'm home. I'm not sleeping on rocks or in a tree or in a cave," replied JW. "It was more than enough." Seeing the concern in her eyes, he smiled. "What's the plan for today?"

"Depends on whom you ask. The men all want to go golfing and talk business. Your grandmother wants you to stay here and talk to her."

"And you?"

A soft smile appeared on her face.

"You're home and not in a tree or in a cave. That's enough for me. What do you want to do?"

"For starters? Coffee. Oh, and where did Parker crash?"

"He's next door. Would he have slept through the Franklin hurri—"

"Right here," JW's partner appeared in the doorway with a broad grin. "Was that the city version of roosters?"

Zoey laughed.

"Wait until Nick and Henry get in this afternoon," she said in reference to her two youngest nephews. "Chaos will absolutely reign this weekend."

"Definitely coffee," muttered JW. "Lots of coffee. We're golfing today, Parker."

"Are the clubs I used last time still here?" the spotter inquired. Zoey nodded. "Sweet. Let's go."

The two laughed at JW's groan.

"Oh, and Grant and Bron planned something for tonight. The younger ones weren't thrilled but were promised to get you the rest of the weekend."

"Planned? What did they plan?" wondered JW.

"I believe copious amounts of alcohol are involved," replied his mother dryly. "Bron called it a bacchanalia. If you don't have swim trunks, I suggest you acquire them by five."

"Here?" JW could not see anything getting out of hand anywhere near his grandparents.

"Not here," she told him, "at the Livingston manor."

"Sean's home?" JW tilted his head. "I thought he was doing a European tour or something."

"Wait," Parker held up a hand, "as in Sean Livingston? The actor/singer?"

"Yup," Zoey confirmed. "He's recovering from food poisoning." She rolled her eyes. "I'm not sure the doctors would recommend alcohol consumption as treatment, but then I'm old-fashioned." With a wink at her son, she strolled to the door and gave

Parker a hug. "Better hurry or Grant and Bron will drink all the coffee."

"Like hell," JW vowed, flipping the covers back.

***

The next morning, JW woke at sunrise despite a hangover from hell. Groaning, he took the aspirin he'd left on the table at the side of the bed, rolled over and managed two more hours of sleep. After waking some time later and swallowing two more white tablets, he took a shower, pulled on jeans and a black cotton T-shirt, and slowly made his way to the morning room.

His younger cousins, grandmother and Aunt Talia, Nick and Nora's mother, were already seated at the long table. His gaze swept the room a second time as he walked to the sideboard for coffee.

"Where's Mom?"

"She's at her class," Gisele replied.

"What class?"

He poured the coffee, wrinkling his nose. Dainty cup and not nearly strong enough.

"Some class on self-defense or waving your arms around," Talia sniffed.

"Ah," JW nodded, sipping the coffee. *Nope, not tough enough.*

"I tried to tell her to cancel," his grandmother replied in a lofty tone, "or get someone to take it over, but she refused."

Behind their grandmother's back, Gisele met his gaze then rolled her eyes.

"She said after the party last night, you'd be recovering until she got back anyway."

"I'll be fine in a couple hours," he commented, sitting between Nora and Penny.

"That's when she should be back," Penny, the youngest of the cousins, told him quietly.

"Mom's good at those things," agreed JW, studying her. "You okay?"

"Stop fussing over the girl," snapped his grandmother. "Good heavens, there's no need to go into—"

"Are you still riding?" JW asked Penny. "When is your next competition? Will I be able to see you?"

A flush of pleasure colored her cheeks as she nodded. Casting a worried glance at the matriarch, she bit her lower lip.

"It's next weekend. At Madison Square Garden."

"Then make sure I can be front and center," he told her. "Promise?"

The joy in her expression was enough to chase away the last banging in his head. The only child of his grandmother's niece, Penny's guardianship was divided and she was forced to alternate her homes between the Franklins and her father's family the Davidsons. There was little stability or security in her life.

Taking a break from finishing her thesis until his mother came home, Giselle was quite happy to catch him up on the gossip while the younger ones did races in the pool. Ever alert, even at home, JW listened with half an ear. *Wait. What?*

"What was that about Ally Brown?"

"She's disappeared," Giselle repeated, slathering sunscreen on her legs. "In a way, I don't blame her after the way MacLauren treated her. It's one thing to have it in legal paperwork, but to discuss it so publicly?" Shaking her head, she sent her blonde ponytail whipping about her. "All of which makes me think the problem was more him than her."

"Something along the lines of protesting too much?" he muttered.

"Exactly," she agreed. "He didn't need to humiliate her like that. I went to see her on Christmas Eve and she couldn't even stand up."

"That upset?" JW frowned, not liking to think of Ally so distraught. *Christmas Eve. That's when I found out she had married him.*

"That drunk," Gisele corrected. "After a couple weeks, David finally locked the liquor cabinet and insisted she see a therapist."

"Who did she go to?"

"Dr. Jones."

"Tim Jones?" JW questioned. *Tim's a member of the Shadows. David would trust him with Ally.*

"That's the one," she nodded, stretching out on the lounger. "Even without having been married to the asshole . . ." Green eyes flicked around to check on which family members were within earshot. "Don't tell Grandmother I said that."

"Lips are sealed," he promised with a smile.

"Even without the annulment, she's been through so much that she probably needed to talk to someone anyway." Giselle sipped her water. "I saw her in mid-April, and she seemed so much happier. Then . . ." she shook her head, "she disappeared. Grant mentioned it and Grandmother sniffed that she probably wasn't sophisticated enough for the city and went back to the coastal town she's from."

"Considering how things have gone for her in the city, you can't blame her," JW commented.

"No, but I wish she'd told me where she was going," Gisele pouted. "That's what friends are for."

"You can't tell where she is?"

If Gisele concentrated, she could find people. It had always made games of hide-and-seek interesting. Whomever had irritated her the most would be completely ignored. Even if she didn't want to admit it, Gisele had that characteristic from their grandmother in spades. Now, he could tell the answer from her grumpy expression before she spoke.

"Not a thing. And it's odd," she frowned, "because I could before. I could feel how he treated her, JW." She started crying. "The things he said to her were so cruel, so horrible. What he did to her that last day was—"

Holding her, JW tried to tamp down the anger at MacLauren. Instead, his mind turned to other things. Given what Gisele could do, there were only a few people who might be able to block her from finding someone. There were five in Ireland or England, but only three in the states. Fairly certain his mother wouldn't have, that left

Liam and his father Paddy. *Well, I was planning on going anyway. Now, I know who to look for.*

Mentioning it to Parker as Giselle settled back on the lounger, he saw his friend's gaze slide sideways before he said something about him and Bron challenging Nick and Henry to tricks on the billiard table. Following the man's eyes, JW saw only Gisele, stretched out on the chaise. Parker walked away and JW frowned. He trusted the man with his life without questioning, but with his cousin?

    ***

Backing his truck into a space in the club's underground garage that evening, JW turned the engine off and got out. Patting the hood, he grinned. His grandmother had fussed about a Franklin driving such a vehicle. *It's sixteen years old. Surely you can get something newer. Maybe we could get you one for Christmas?* Zoey, knowing green eyes sending a message to her son to get out, had promptly changed the conversation in a way guaranteed to distract the matriarch.

Chuckling to himself, he imagined his mother had used the argument as a way to distract herself from the knowledge that she'd helped her son escape to a sex club for which she was a board member. *Yeah, let's not think about that. That's definitely in the ick column, as Heather would put it.*

Walking to the elevator, he tapped in his five-digit code. The sequence alerted security as to who was entering, as well as automatically determined his access to different floors. For now though, once the doors slid open, he simply pressed the button for the main floor. He'd make an appearance in the Pub. If he knew Liam the way he thought he did, he knew what his distant cousin would be doing.

A drink, talk to a few people, then up to the selection room.

What he didn't expect was to see Liam standing in the corridor when the doors opened again.

"About time you showed up," was his only greeting.

Stepping out, JW grinned as they embraced, thumping each other's backs.

"Drink first?" Liam asked.

"That was the plan."

"Thought so."

"Will you stop that," JW complained as they walked along the corridor to the muted sounds of Gaelic music and conversation. "Isn't it considered very rude to read family members' minds?"

"Probably," Liam admitted. "But sometimes your thoughts are so damn loud, it's hard to block them."

"Mm, block harder then," JW suggested, giving him a meaningful glance.

"Gisele is quite persistent," Liam muttered. "I never know when she would try."

"I'll bet." JW grinned at his cousin's strength and abilities.

"Master JW, Master Liam," the bartender greeted them quietly, setting two glasses of whiskey on the mahogany bar.

"Thank you, Smithers," JW nodded.

Glasses in hand, they did a circuit around the room, talking to other members. Finally, Liam glanced at his watch.

"Upstairs," he stated.

"About time," JW muttered.

Passing the bar, they put their mostly untouched glasses on the wood. JW stayed silent, feeling the anticipation and his cock rise.

"This is her first time in the Selection Room," Liam said quietly, once they were alone in the elevator.

"What?" JW's breath caught.

"She just finished her training yesterday." Liam hesitated, and that had JW's hackles rising. "MacLauren did quite a number on her, JW. I almost didn't take her in."

"I'll take care of her," he vowed.

"I know. Will you let her take care of you?" Liam wondered in a mild voice.

JW smirked as the doors slid open and they strode down the corridor.

"I'm sure she'll do just fine with that."

As Liam pushed the door open, JW heard the rustling as waiting submissives dropped to their knees and sat back on their heels. Their heads were bowed by the time JW had entered and closed the door.

And nearly swallowed his tongue when his eyes found her. Her hour-glass figure seemed to shimmer under the translucent silver robe. *Control. Control. You are the Master. Maintain control.* His dick was already hard and ready to play. *Screw control. Let's screw her.* Even as he moved slowly toward her, Liam moved behind the line, tapping each man or woman on the head and murmuring for them to leave. By the time he reached Ally, Liam was leaving as well.

JW stopped in front of her and could see how she trembled. *Good. She should be nervous.*

Ally tried to stay still, but her body wouldn't listen. She could hear Master Liam and waited to be tapped as well. The door opened and closed again and the toes of black boots stopped just beyond her knees. *Me? Why me? No, no, you've made a mistake, sir. It's my first time in the selection room. You don't want me, sir.*

The boots didn't move. The Master didn't speak. She was so edgy that her body swayed.

Strong hands gripped her upper arms, and she was hauled to her feet. Except her feet never touched the floor as she was held against a hard, lean muscled body.

"I should spank that ass of yours until you can't sit down for a month," a growl rumbled in her ear.

Breaking every protocol, she jerked her head up and stared.

"JW," she breathed.

"And another month for that," he added, eyes narrowing before she remembered to drop her chin.

"How are you, sir?" she whispered, even as her pussy clenched. Her breasts were already tightening, swelling as if he was touching them. *How did he know I was here?*

"I have you for twelve hours, Ally," he told her. "At the end of that time, we are both going to be so exhausted we can't move." Now, her feet carefully touched down. His hands smoothed over her shoulders and framed her face. "And I will make sure you understand that it was his fault. Not yours."

"Sir?" she breathed. *He knows! Oh, God, he knows.* Humiliated, her hands covered her face as she stepped away. "Oh, God, no."

He followed her, wrapped an arm around her waist, and lifted her against him again.

"How could you have been with him?" he demanded. "After that kiss?"

"Well, let's see," she fired back, her head coming up as she glared. "You disappeared without a word, as if the kiss didn't mean a thing to you. You left me on the bench. I looked for you and you were gone." Sulking, she pouted. "You knew I was with David and Diana. You could have written a quick note or something. I would have written back. Waited to see what happened if that's what you wanted to do."

"I've held onto that kiss. That memory." Stunned, she could only gape at him. "I've dreamt of what I'd do to you." He set her down so swiftly she stumbled. "Get your cloak or I'll fuck you here and now."

Stunned at the idea, she rushed to the hook where a lone cloak hung. Swirling it around her shoulders, she moved quickly to where he waited by the door. Ally pulled the hood up to cover her face as she followed him down the hall. Hands clasped tightly before her, she kept her eyes on the floor.

And plowed right into his broad back when she didn't see him stop.

"Sorry, sir," she gasped, unable to believe she'd screwed up already. Then she compounded the mistake by looking up into his eyes as he turned around to face her. He may never grace magazine covers, but there was something about his face that appealed to her. His skin was tanned from sun exposure and the fingers that had held her chin were callused.

"One spanking," he murmured, his hand coming up and touching her collar. "Should I make it two?" She dropped her eyes and he grunted. "I gave newbies fresh out of basic a chance. I can do the same with you."

As he punched his code into the panel near the door, relief sweep through Ally's body. Now, if she could pay attention, she might make it through the next twelve hours with her ass intact. The thought of him spanking then fucking her had heat gathering in her core. She knew her pussy would be dripping soon. His fingers wrapped around her upper arm and propelled her into the room ahead of him.

Startled, she whirled about to face him. Striding toward her as the door slid closed behind him, he pulled the cloak from her shoulders before removing the barrette that held her long hair back at her nape.

"Kneel, Ally."

Knowing what was coming, she obeyed but did not sit back on her heels. His hands went to his belt.

"May I, sir?" she whispered.

"Yes," he replied, moving his hands away.

She quickly worked the buckle, moving the ends back a loop before releasing the button and easing the zipper down. He shoved his slacks and briefs down. She inhaled. His cock was semi-erect, but she could tell that it would be larger than those she'd been exposed to during the past six weeks.

"May I touch you, sir?" Ally asked hesitantly.

"Absolutely."

Wrapping her fingers at the root, she stroked his shaft, loving the velvety smoothness. His fingers weaved through her hair as her touch brought him fully erect. She was doing this. She aroused a man. The thrill gave her more confidence.

"Open your mouth."

She heard the hoarseness as his lust grew.

Obediently, she parted her lips and tilted her head back, ready for his cock as a baby bird would accept food. His length pressed past her lips and over her tongue. When she flicked her tongue over the slit, he groaned. His grip on her head tightened. That quickly, he took total control.

He stroked his cock in and out, going so deep she would have gagged if he'd stayed there long. Ally had let her hands fall to her sides when he'd ordered her to open her mouth. Now, she lightly ran her palms up the backs of his muscular thighs and gripped his taut buttocks.

"Come on," he muttered.

Puzzled, she peeked up at his face. His eyes were closed and it almost looked like he was in pain. Not sure what to do, she lowered her hands from his ass. With a moan, he pulled his cock out of her mouth. The pressure of his hands on her head brought her to her feet and she stood uneasily, uncertain.

"Look at me, Ally," he told her, fingers flying down the front of his shirt to push the buttons free. "Unless I say otherwise, you are to watch my face. Learn my expressions. Watch and pay attention."

"Yes, sir," she replied, surprised at such an unorthodox command.

He quickly bent and loosened the laces of his boots then tugged them off. In seconds, he was naked. Disobeying him slightly, she glanced up and down his nude body. Powerful, lean muscles covered the body nearly a foot taller than her own five-three. Dark hair sprinkled his pecs, narrowing into a thin line over rippling abs past his navel to his . . . she gaped at the thick cock already jutting out from the dark hair of his groin and darted her eyes back to his face.

A slight smile curved his lips briefly. A hint of approval warred with the lust in his eyes. Reaching forward, he tugged on the ribbon that held her toga up. It pooled around her feet. She couldn't control the tremors that swept through her as she maintained eye contact with him. The way he looked at her made her think he wanted to devour her from head to toe.

"Turn around," he whispered, gesturing his hand in a circle. "Let me see you."

Obeying, she spun fully around, wondering if the rasp in his voice meant that he was trying to control himself. Could he really want her that much? She'd read romance novels and had dreamt of a man so eager and desperate for her that he would . . .

Wrapping his long fingers around her arm, he practically dragged her to the bed. He stopped and her momentum whipped her around to face him.

With an arm around her waist, he held her to his chest and gazed down at her for a long moment. With his other hand in her hair, Ally could do nothing but stare at him. As the hand at her back moved, his mouth came down on hers.

She moaned, pressing her body against his, wanting more of his touch than she could believe. His hand went between her thighs. With no preliminary exploration, his fingers thrust inside her pussy. She whimpered in need as her inner walls clutched at his fingers.

Almost immediately, he ended the kiss, his eyes narrowed. He threw her on the bed and followed her so quickly that she was still trying to figure out what had happened when his heavy body loomed over her. His hands pulled her thighs apart, making room for his narrow hips, and he thrust his cock inside her pussy.

She gasped as he pushed her knees to her shoulders. He stretched her. He filled her. And he fucked her as if his life depended on it.

This was what she'd been looking for. A man taking control of her, making her take his cock, heating her blood, doing what he wanted to her. It was like nothing she'd experienced before. *It's because it's him,* some part of her mind whispered.

The pounding of his hips became faster, deeper, and harder, accented by his deepening grunts. She closed her eyes and lost herself in the heat that filled her core. This man had chosen her. He wanted her. He was using her and was relishing the use of her pussy. Friction built up. Heat rose up in her. Ally felt as if a coil of electricity was winding tighter in her belly, eager to be released. She barely remembered in time.

"Sir?" she pleaded in a whisper.

His eyes met hers and must have recognized her need.

"No, not yet," he grunted.

Denied an orgasm, Ally fought for control. He had said "no." She'd never been denied before and now she struggled not to throw her head back and scream in pleasure. *He chose me,* she chanted silently. She would obey him completely. She would please him and then, maybe, he would let her come before the twelve hours were up.

Her training came back to her—focus on the Dom. He'd said she could look at him, and she drank in her fill of a man, finally, enjoying sex with her. His arms were roped muscles on either side of her head. His deep chest and broad shoulders glistened with sweat and his breathing was fast and shallow. Nearly as fast as the thrusts of his cock into her pussy. His head lowered to his chest as if everything in him was focused on his efforts. He lifted his chin slightly and met her gaze. Lust blazed in his green eyes.

"Squeeze my cock," his hoarse voice told her. "Squeeze hard. Now."

Holding her breath, she tightened her pussy around his cock. Suddenly, she wanted him inside her as far and deep as he could go. And she didn't want him to leave.

"Master, use me," she whispered, not sure if he could hear her over his grunts.

"Yes!" he groaned in triumph.

He thrust one last time and released inside her, his hips pressed tightly against her core. Ally felt the hot rush into her body and smiled to herself. His heavy body collapsed and she sighed under his weight. Wrapping her arms and legs around his torso, she hummed softly. He had found satisfaction in her body.

For a long moment, the only sound was his heavy breathing.

"Should I spank you for not paying attention earlier or reward you for not coming?" he murmured.

Ally felt herself flush at the reminders, both embarrassed at her mistake and proud from his praise. Master JW raised himself slightly, bracing his weight on an elbow near her ear.

"I think...both," he decided, a finger tracing her collarbone. "I can't have you making mistakes, but I also enjoy your obedience."

"Yes, sir," she whispered, hoping he'd go easy on her since she had obeyed him.

His fingers plucked at her nipples, teasing them until they were pebbled and erect. A whimper slipped from her lips. His low chuckle surprised her.

"Perhaps I can punish and reward you at the same time."

She frowned and dared to look swiftly at his mouth without meeting his eyes. His lips were curved slightly. His fingers pinched her nipple and she inhaled sharply. He pinched the other and nodded.

"Yes, I think I can," he murmured, lifting his hips from hers and pulling his cock from her aching pussy.

He left the bed and stalked to the chest of drawers near the door. Knowing better than to move until he told her to, Ally twisted her head to watch his movement across the room. He turned. Seeing the objects he had selected, she understood what he intended.

His large hands held a flogger, nipple clamps, a small tube, and a condom packet. Returning to the bed, he bent over her chest and suckled her breasts. Moaning and arching into his mouth, she struggled to remain still. When he lifted his head, she watched his expressions: intent, serious, and confident. A thrill rippled through her. Her master knew what she needed. He was watching her, playing her, just as Mistress Alice, the submissive's trainer, had told her a good Dominant would. Ally felt part of her mind relax as she drifted into a deeper bond of trust with him.

The nipple clamps locked on her now turgid tips, and he tightened them until she cried out at the pressure. She took a deep breath as her body adjusted and the coil of heat grew in her belly. Her hips arched slightly off the bed.

"Master," she whispered, hearing the hunger in her own voice.

"All fours, head near the pillows," he ordered tersely.

She scrambled to obey, keeping her eyes focused on the muted brown pattern of the bedspread. She felt his eyes on her body and failed to prevent the shiver that ran through her limbs. His hand smoothed over her back, sweeping her hair aside so it hung over her left shoulder.

"Knees farther apart," he told her.

She opened her thighs up several more inches. The first strike of the leather strips was light on the backs of her thighs. She closed her eyes, knowing he tested himself as much as her.

"Four more," he said quietly. "Then I'll fuck your ass."

"Yes, sir," she replied softly. "Thank you, sir."

The leather struck higher, just below her pussy. She gasped at the pain that lanced through her lower body. The next fell even harder at the curve of her ass. She couldn't bite back the sob that left her throat. The third and fourth were progressively harder and landed in the same area as the second. Her ass throbbed and she reveled in the fire that filled her womb. Ever since Master Liam had administered her first spanking, she'd realized that she would do almost anything to get one. The sting on her ass never failed to push the fire in her pussy to new heights.

"Damn," he muttered, his hands stroking her fiery ass. "You've a beautiful ass, Ally." He leaned over her, the heat of his body adding to the fire inside her. His arms pulled her slightly to the side of the bed where he stood. His breath was hot in her ear. "My cock is hard from how well you took your spanking, which means I've got to fuck you again."

She heard him rip open the condom packet and knew that, when he rolled it over his dick, he would fuck her again. In the ass.

The bed dipped as he climbed on and then everything went still for a moment. She squealed slightly as a generous amount of cold lube hit her anus. Ally closed her eyes, her fingers curling around the bedspread as his fingers began pressing into her tight rosette.

She'd never had anal sex willingly before coming to the Shadows, never even considered it. During training, she'd had butt plugs inserted of increasingly longer and wider sizes. But no one had ever taken her in the ass. *I trust Master JW*, she reminded herself. He was taking care of her. He was paying attention to her body's responses and being careful with her. She wriggled her ass at him.

He caught her hips and held her still.

"Do not come," he told her gruffly.

"Yes, sir," she whispered as she felt the latex-covered tip of his dick slide between her ass cheeks.

He pushed in, quickly pushing past the tight resistance offered by her sphincter muscles and thrusting deep. She moaned at the fiery invasion. He felt bigger than the training plugs, but, thankfully, not as hard. Oh, God, she felt full!

"All right?"

She smiled to herself, hearing the concern for her in his voice. Yet, there was also need. A need to fuck her where no one else had. Did he know that?

"Ally?"

"Oh, yes, sir! I'm all right, sir."

His hands gripped her hips as he pounded in and out of her. Gasping, Ally opened her eyes and looked down between her legs.

His thighs filled the gap between hers and she marveled at the differences. Hers were hairless and lightly muscled from the physical conditioning the Shadows required of submissives and slaves. His were cords of strength with rough dark hair sprinkled near his hips and more near his knees.

One of his hands snaked around her hip and played with her clit. She caught her breath and threw her head back, unable to believe how hungry for an orgasm she was. How much more did he expect her to take? He thrust in until his hips ground against her cheeks and she whimpered in need.

"Master, please," she begged, keeping her voice soft and low.

"Shh, little one," he murmured, his hands caressing her ass and lower back.

He pulled his cock out of her ass. Seconds later, the condom dropped onto the nightstand to her right. His hands grabbed her hips and he drove his cock into her pussy before she even realized what he was doing. She cried out, knowing she was closer to coming, desperate to be given permission. Her walls clenched around him, frantically trying to keep him inside. Panting, she writhed despite his grip on her. He stroked in and out of her wet heat several times.

"Master, please. I'm so close," she begged.

One arm whipped around her waist and pulled her up so quickly that her head fell back against his shoulder. His palm pressed against her stomach before moving down and pinching her clit. Fire shot through her pussy, forcing the delicate muscles to clench and squeeze around his rigid cock.

"Sir!"

His other hand tangled in her hair and forced her head back so he could see her face.

"Come for me," he ordered, his fingers tweaking the nub again.

Panting for breath and held helplessly against his chest, Ally closed her eyes. His cock filled her pussy. Her ass throbbed from the lashes and the size of his shaft. Her nipples pulsed against the clamps and now...

"Stop thinking," he growled, his fingers gripping tighter in her hair. "Come for me. Come hard."

She cried out in need. Her body ached and all she wanted was to come. To experience the orgasm he'd denied her earlier. His mouth covered hers and his tongue thrust past her lips. Moaning as he completely possessed her, Ally felt something inside her snap free.

As he held her tight, her body stiffened, trembling for several seconds as her pussy clutched his cock. Her scream echoed around the room. She closed her eyes and saw stars. She felt light-headed.

He raised his head slightly and she gasped for breath.

"Oh, dear God," she breathed. "I think my heart stopped."

"Good girl," he murmured, arms cradling her limp body.

"Thank you, master," she panted, eyes still closed as her head lolled against his shoulder.

"I'm going to fuck you hard, Ally. Hard and fast."

He shoved her shoulders down and she pressed herself into the pillow. He gripped her hips and pulled nearly completely out of her heat. *No! I want him inside. Only inside. Taking me.*

"Sir! Please, fuck me!" she begged, opening her eyes and daring to look over her shoulder at him. "Please!"

"That's it," he nodded in approval. "Beg me."

"Please, please, please…"

He drove into her weeping core and she moaned. If she'd thought he'd fucked her ass hard and deep, it had been just a sample of how this man liked things. All she could do was hold onto the pillow as he took her.

Her second orgasm came out of nowhere, slamming into her so hard and fast that she pushed up off the bed with a scream as her pussy pulsed around him. Falling back down, she gasped for breath.

"Not done," he grunted, still hammering into her pulsing flesh. "And neither are you."

Shocked, she forced the sweaty strands of hair out of the way so she could see his face.

"Sir?" she whispered, gazing up at his enigmatic expression.

"Squeeze my cock with your sweet pussy, Ally," he told her. "As if your life depended on it."

JW had no idea what possessed him. Rather, he didn't want to think about it. He saw a flash of uncertainty and what nearly looked like fear in the dark eyes staring at him over a creamy shoulder. Yes, she would be worried now, despite that kiss months ago. She was a relatively new submissive picked by a Dom clearly close to the Shadows's owner. What he really wanted wasn't *entirely* a submissive. He just wanted to fuck himself and her, if he could, into utter exhaustion.

No tricks, no more props, just his cock in her mouth, pussy, and ass until he'd wrung himself completely dry.

And she responded so perfectly to him. That heart-shaped ass had striped beautifully, and he'd watched as moisture had pearled and dripped from her pussy. For a brief moment, he let himself imagine giving her daily spankings, sometimes to remind her who was in control and other times because she'd broken one of his rules. Then, with discipline done, he would fuck her wherever they were. She'd grow hotter and wilder the rougher he used her. She didn't know her own limits. He would take her beyond…

He clenched his jaw and buried such imaginings to the deepest corners of his mind. He would not, could not, consider anything permanent or lasting. He would enjoy this time with Ally and not think about the future.

"I'll have to tell Liam to give you a long rest when I'm done with you," he whispered harshly.

Done with you echoed in her mind. Firmly reminding her of who and what she was. Ally set that aside. David had been right to suggest Shadows might be a solution. She *did* have a sexual drive. Kevin hadn't done anything to get a response from her. Of course, she admitted, as Master JW turned her over and fondled her breasts, after being kissed by him any man would have had a hard time getting any reaction out of her.

Ally woke with a start in her own twin bed on the submissives' level of the club. She lifted her head and winced as every muscle in her body screamed from use and fatigue. With a groan, she dropped her head back on the pillow. Flat on her back, she stared at the ceiling.

"You're awake. I must tell Master Liam."

Slowly, she managed to turn her head, catching a glimpse of one of the slaves leaving the room. Sighing, she rolled to her left side to face the door and carefully brought her legs even to her waist and tried get her brain working.

Moments later, the door opened and she gasped at the sight of Master Liam entering.

"Master Liam," she stammered, forcing her body out of the bed to kneel next to it.

"Easy, Ally," he said soothingly. He caught her before she could get to her knees, scooped her up, and returned her to the bed. He pulled the blanket up over her shoulders. "You've more than earned a rest. You may look at me for this talk. How are you feeling? Do you have any questions?"

"Sir?" Her eyes tracked his movements as he fetched the lone straight-back chair from the small desk and brought it to the side of the bed. "How long was I asleep?"

"Nearly twelve hours," he told her, amusement in his voice. She moaned and closed her eyes but he just chuckled. "Not to worry. JW was more than pleased with you. He said you were exactly what he needed."

"Really?" Her spirits picked up at that and she opened her eyes.

Master Liam leaned back in the chair and crossed one leg so the ankle rested on the opposite knee.

"Really," he confirmed. "I'll admit that I had my doubts when David suggested we train you as a submissive. Coming from any sort of abusive relationship isn't necessarily the best entrance into this lifestyle. It doesn't matter if the abuse was mental, emotional, or physical." He studied Ally's face and she dropped her eyes to the sheets. "You did very well, Ally. Very well."

"Thank you, Master Liam," Ally replied softly, relief flooding through her.

"JW said he fucked you hard, so I don't want you in the selection room until you're fully rested. The doctor will be by in three days. He'll check you out and make sure you've completely recovered."

"Yes, Master Liam," she whispered.

Getting up, he put the chair back before coming to stand by the bed. "You pleased me as well, Ally. JW is a good friend of mine. Thank you for taking care of him."

He turned and was at the door before she managed to speak.

"Master Liam?"

"Yes?" He paused, hand on the door, and looked over his shoulder.

"I wondered…" she started slowly. "…do you think he may come to the Shadows again? Soon?"

She was certain the hope in her voice and expression were clear for Master Liam to see. Master Liam gave her a look she didn't even try to figure out.

"He's returned to duty, Ally," he said quietly. "I don't know when he'll be back."

"What? I didn't get to say good-bye," she fretted, biting her bottom lip.

"Ally, look at me."

Immediately she obeyed the stern voice.

"Focus on healing yourself. You can't help anyone now or in the future if you're not strong enough." He smiled. "I know that sounds odd—"

"In the garden that night," she murmured, too lost in her thoughts to see his frown at her interruption. "Bron and Nick were talking. I didn't quite understand what they meant."

"What did they say?" Liam asked quietly.

"Something about how Nick had felt the pain and fear of people on 9/11. And their grandmother didn't seem to like that he could."

Liam snorted slightly.

"No, she doesn't," he muttered under his breath, then smiled at her puzzled expression. "Take care of yourself, Ally. You need to be strong."

Before she could react or ask another question, he was gone.

Relaxing back against the pillows, Ally considered what had been said, and what hadn't.

Chapter Six

Cleared by the doctor, Ally joined the other subs in the selection room three days later. Before any Doms or Dommes were expected, the red eye of the camera in the corner was off and Mistress Alice had yet to join them to supervise any selections. The submissives relaxed and chatted.. Many of them were comparing notes on different masters and mistresses.

"Three days off?" one of the senior submissives murmured. "Master Liam must have received a very good report from the master who chose you."

"I think he did," Ally replied, smiling shyly at Rosa. "The master was certainly, um, very thorough."

"A good first time is always a good thing," Frank, a male submissive told her. "It helps you feel more settled."

"I don't know about settled," Ally sighed. "But I was so exhausted, I don't remember how I got to my room."

The other seven submissives chuckled. The door opened and they all dropped to their knees, bowing their heads. Ally peeked and saw brown loafers. Filled with disappointment, she didn't react when the shoes stopped in front of her.

"I said 'I choose you'," the harsh voice rasped.

A hand grabbed her upper right arm and she was hauled to her feet. Stunned, she saw his face and froze in fear. From the first day of training, she'd heard about this Dom. How the slaves cowered when he entered their selection room. How he'd beaten a submissive so badly she'd had to be taken to the emergency room.

"Master Madison," Rosa spoke up. "Ally is new perhaps—"

"Shut up," he snarled at her. "I choose her."

"No," Ally whispered. Now, Ally used the one power a submissive had: she could say no. "No," she stated firmly and loudly so all in the room could witness her denial. "I do not agree."

"I don't give a shit," he laughed, dragging her toward the door.

"No," she shouted, trying to brace her feet to slow him down. "I do not agree."

"You don't have a fucking choice," he sneered.

"I do not agree," she protested.

Madison had her in the hallway.

"Let me go," Ally shouted, now trying to pry his fingers off her arm. "Let me go! I do not agree."

Desperate, she kicked out as he dragged her beside him, hitting the side of his knee and making him stumble.

"Oh, that will cost you," Madison snarled.

Struggling to free her forearm, she never saw the fist that punched her left temple. Limp, she collapsed to her knees as he swung again. She crashed against the wall.

"Bad master," shouted the submissives from the selection room as they rushed down the hall. "Bad master, bad master."

Trying to stay conscious, Ally heard doors opening as masters and mistresses responded to the call. But the submissives reached her first. Two of the male subs swarmed over Madison as the women wrapped their arms around her and pulled her away. In the chaos, she slumped in Rosa's arms as blackness took over.

Two days later, understanding the terms *bruised* and *battered* all too well, Ally sat in Master Liam's office. Keeping her eyes lowered, she felt him studying her.

"From an excellent start to a nightmare," he murmured in disgust. "For the moment, protocols are relaxed, Ally. I need your reactions."

Nodding, she lifted her chin and stayed silent.

"While I'm working the contracts to properly evict Madison from this club, he has been banned from the submissives floors."

"The slaves?" she fretted, twisting her hands on her lap. "Won't he take that out on them?"

"Don't worry. I'm keeping an eye on them, Ally," he reassured in a determined tone.

"David said you did," she whispered, smiling slightly.

"I can understand if you want to leave, though I'll regret it very much," he added. "While I was concerned about your reasons, I think you do make a very good submissive."

His praise made her smile.

"Thank you, Master Liam. I'd like to stay. I'm not sure how comfortable I'd be returning to the selection room right away. The nightmare is too recent."

"Very understandable," he answered. "I'll put you in the demonstration rooms. Only for what you've already agreed to. If, as you become more familiar with other aspects and are perhaps more interested in them, you have only to tell Mistress Alice."

"Thank you, Master Liam," she replied, relaxing. "Mistress Alice has been very supportive and comforting. As have the other submissives." Something had been worrying her and lifted her head slightly. "May I ask a question?"

"Certainly."

"The other submissives, the ones who saved me, they won't be punished, will they? Especially Frank and Timmy, since they put their hands on a master and—"

"Don't worry, Ally," Liam chuckled. "Frank and Timmy will certainly not be punished. In fact, I think they're worn out from their newfound celebrity. I may need to ration their time in the selection room as they've been so popular."

"Frank will love that," she giggled, then ducked her head. "Sorry. Was that out of line?"

"That's fine, Ally," he murmured. "It's good to see you interacting with the others."

Encouraged, yet knowing she was stepping even further into forbidden territory, she took a deep breath.

"What's your question, Ally?"

"Master JW," she wondered, lifting her head enough to see his face. "Do you think he'll return soon?"

Because she was watching, she saw the concern and worry in his expression before the serious mask of the senior master reappeared.

"He's a soldier, Ally," he told her quietly. "He flew out the day after he left here." A brief smile flashed across his face. "I was told that he seemed rather," his green eyes flitted to her, "relaxed, shall we say? Despite being called back so soon after starting his leave." Happily, she smiled back even as he became solemn again. "Focus on yourself, Ally. Find your own strength and goals. Your own purpose. Only then will you have the strength to help and support others."

Puzzled, she frowned. *That's the second time he's said that.* "Sir?"

Without answering, he tapped at his keyboard, then glanced at her.

"I've told Mistress Alice about your change in status."

Understanding she'd been dismissed, Ally stood and bent her upper body forward slightly in respect.

"Thank you, sir."

Ally felt as if she was being stalked. Every time she entered a demonstration room, Madison was there, sitting in the front row and leaning forward with an evil glint in his eyes. Mistress Alice tried but failed to get the board to ban him from any room a submissive occupied. In response, she and two other mistresses had taken Ally under their personal protection.

"One of the very bad things about having a family in absolute control of something," she muttered, coiling the rope. "Padraig the third should not have decided that each branch of his children should be represented. It gives bad seeds too much control and the good too little in limiting their damage."

"What did the board say, mistress?" Ally wondered as she stood on the other side of the table folding the silk binding cloths.

"They basically all took his side," she fumed. "Except for Paddy, Liam, and Zoey, of course."

"Zoey?" Ally blinked. That was not a very common name. Mistress Alice *couldn't* mean who she thought she did.

"Zoey Franklin," came the blithe confirmation. "Her paternal grandmother was Padraig's great-granddaughter. Master Paddy nominated her years ago and the members approved her presence, thinking she'd just do whatever they told her to if she showed up to meetings at all."

"That doesn't sound like the Zoey Franklin I met once," Ally murmured. "It was only a few moments, but still."

"Oh, they probably quickly regretted it," Mistress Alice chuckled, moving on to the next and last rope. "Zoey Franklin, thank God, has a mind of her own and is incorruptible. If she takes something on, she sees it through."

"She was the one who told David the truth about my father," Ally ventured. "No one else would, but she did."

Mistress Alice looked over at her.

"She's a good woman."

"She is," Ally agreed, glancing up with a smile.

The others didn't seem to resent that she was only allowed in the demonstration rooms. Everyone understood what Madison had done. Breaking a submissive's trust or ignoring their right to reject a master was not taken lightly. *By everyone except the board,* she sighed, closing her eyes to avoid seeing Madison's smirking face as Master Liam began the session.

As summer kicked into full steam, tension seemed to stretch members of the club tight. The first anniversary of the 9/11 attacks approached and, while New Yorkers were determined to carry on with life, the trauma was still so new. Soon after the Fourth of July, Ally was summoned to Master Liam's office.

"Sit down, Ally," he instructed mildly. "Look at me."

Silently she obeyed, startled at the instruction. It was hard to keep her chin up under his scrutiny.

"Do you want to return to the selection room?" His voice finally broke the silence.

"Part of me wants to," she replied quietly. "I know that's why I'm here, but— I guess I should try. I cannot let what happened scare me away from my purpose."

Approval appeared in his eyes before it was replaced with brief concern. "Well, your purpose may not be fully revealed yet. We'll see how it goes."

The next week, Ally used her safe word to end a scene. After it happened the second time, she wasn't surprised to be summoned to

Master Liam's office. Saying a safe word once would arouse concern, but twice in one week had earned her an audience.

She entered quietly once he responded to her timid knock. Closing the door, she knelt and waited for Master Liam to speak. *I just don't know how to explain either time.*

"Ally, did Master Paul harm you?"

"No, sir," she whispered.

"Did Master Jarrett?"

"No, sir."

"Yet, you used your safe word with both of them," he pointed out. She heard a tapping sound as if he was hitting a pen or pencil on his desk. "They both described what they were doing, and the scenes were well within your previously established boundaries."

"Yes, sir."

"So, what was the problem?" Again, she heard the concern without anger.

"I'm not sure, sir," she replied, struggling to find the words. She was relieved that Master Liam didn't seem angry. As David had told her, Master Liam was very protective of the subs and slaves. "I just..." she swallowed and shook her head. "It wasn't them, sir. They didn't hurt me in any way, and they did stop as soon as I said my safe word. That certainly helps with my trust issues. I just— I know what I'm supposed to do, in my head, but..."

"I think I understand, Ally. Madison abused you and that renewed your previous trauma. So now you're questioning what you're doing and why you're here," he said quietly. "I'm going to keep you in the demonstration rooms. When you feel ready for the selection room again, come tell me."

"Yes, sir. Thank you, sir." Relief that he hadn't been angry, that he was giving her a second chance to figure things out, flooded Ally.

"You may leave." As always when he dealt with her, his voice was calm and measured.

"Yes, sir. Thank you, sir."

Ally rose to her feet and left the room. Despite the reprieve, she didn't feel better. She still felt incomplete. And she didn't want to think about the reason.

As she became more secure in her limited role at the Shadows, Ally found new submissives coming to her for advice. To her surprised delight, she realized she'd become a mentor. Being able to help them gave her a shot of confidence. Enough so that, in late August, she screwed up the courage to speak with Master Liam.

"Ally? Are you ready to go back to the selection room?" he asked.

"I don't think so, sir," she replied reluctantly.

"Is there a problem?"

There was a slight bit of curiosity in his voice. As if, despite his awareness of what went on in the club, he was surprised to see her.

"I was wondering…" She took a deep breath. She had to know. Something about Master JW had connected with her. "Has Master JW been back at all? I haven't seen him…I don't know how often he'd be able to come back from wherever and...his mother and cousins were very kind to me and..."

With her eyes on the floor, Ally heard the chair scrape back across the floor. Gasping, she slid out of the chair and dropped to her knees, only to be more stunned when Master Liam crouched next to her.

"Give me your hands, Ally," he said quietly.

Suddenly struggling to breathe, she held out her trembling hands. She knew what that hushed tone meant.

"Did something happen?" Breaking protocol, she lifted her head and met his gaze. She was sure her heart stopped. "What is it?"

"A patrol was ambushed two weeks ago and the leader, a captain, was taken."

"Master JW," she whispered, now clutching at his strong fingers. *He wasn't an officer, was he? Oh, God, no!*

"He and his partner were nearby and responded to the battle. I don't know any of the details, but," Master Liam paused, his fingers tightening on hers, "JW was seriously injured when someone hit an IED. That's something that—"

"I know what it is," gasped Ally, her mind filling with images of the strong body broken and on the ground. "My grandfather and uncle were veterans. They would explain military movies to me. I...is he home? What's happened?"

"He arrived stateside to a military hospital six days ago. His mother stays with him until the hospital staff throws her out and then she probably sneaks in somehow."

Fighting back her fear and not understanding the emotions roiling through her heart, Ally smiled.

"I've met her. I can believe she'd do that." She dared to look at his face. "If you see him, and if no one else is near and you think it appropriate, could you tell him I'm worried for him? That I asked about him?"

"I will," he nodded. "But, Ally, you have to understand that whatever he's been through will have changed him. I don't know how, but I'm sure it has."

"My grandfather was in the Battle of the Bulge," she whispered. "He and his best friend Jack were in a foxhole when their position was overrun. The two fought off a dozen Germans with knives, rocks, and knuckles. When it was over, my grandfather held his best friend in his arms as he died. In Vietnam, my Uncle Jack did three tours."

"Jack," murmured the master.

"For his friend," she nodded. "So, I know how war changes a soldier. How they have to fight each day not to give in to the darkness in their mind."

"And their bodies?" Liam wondered.

"Uncle Jack lost his left leg from the knee down," replied Ally, feeling a chill that had nothing to do with the air conditioning.

Liam studied her a moment and slowly shook his head.

"I'll be damned," he breathed. "Ally, JW has a long road ahead of him. I hope he realizes he needs your strength as much as you need his. But he can be a stubborn cuss."

"We just have to have faith in him," she said softly. "It's all we can do."

"Very true," he agreed, rising easily and bringing her up with him. "And in the meantime, you stay in the demonstration rooms."

"Yes, Master Liam."

****

"You stubborn ass sonuvabitch."

The Boston Brahmin accent cut through a mind fuzzy from whatever the docs were pumping through the IV. JW blinked his eyes open. The man leaning forward on crutches slowly came into focus as he entered the hospital room.

"Ben? Ben! Thank God," he breathed, closing his eyes and relaxing, then snapping them open and struggling to sit fully upright. "Where are we? Parker? The rest of the men?"

"At ease, soldier. We're stateside. At Walter Reed. They're all in rooms up and down the hall," the captain told him, working his way to the side of the bed. "God, JW, I've never been so damn glad to see anyone's ugly mug as I was when you come through that door."

Tears filled his eyes as JW recalled the terror that they wouldn't make it in time. He reached out a hand and Ben took it. No words were needed as both men fought to control their emotions.

"Fuck it," JW muttered. He put his right hand on the slight incline of the mattress and leveraged himself to an upright sitting position. "Come here. I need to make sure you're really alive."

The crutches crashed to the floor as Ben reached for him.

"I thought…" Ben choked, resting his forehead against the older man's shoulder. "I thought I was dead. I fought them, JW. God, I fought with everything I had in me. They interrogated me and I quoted every Bible verse I could remember. I'd yell hallelujah and amen every time they hit me." JW let out a strangled laugh. "Yeah, they didn't like that. Then, when they took me in that room…"

JW's arms tightened around the man as Ben shuddered at the memory of those three days he'd been at the mercy of the enemy.

"We've all seen the videos of what they've done. We know the risks, but to know it's coming," Ben whispered. "I just closed my eyes and prayed. I didn't dare hope for a miracle. I just prayed to God for courage. I prayed that I wouldn't cry and beg for my life. That when they saw it, my family would know that I'd died as bravely as anyone could."

"I was so scared we wouldn't make it," JW told him, voice choked with that terror. "So scared. I told Parker and your men that we had to find you and get your ass home, because we sure as hell didn't want to face your grandmother if we didn't."

Ben barked out a laugh.

"God, she'll love that."

For a long moment, neither spoke. They didn't move, holding each other, resting their foreheads against shoulders—simply relieved to be alive.

"What's happening out in the real world?" JW finally wondered.

"They're trying to court-martial everyone who came after me," Ben told him.

Lifting his head, JW stared at Ben and it hit him. *More than fifteen fucking years and they want to what?*

"What? We saved your ass and they want to punish us for it?"

"Some three-star is playing politics," Ben shook his head. "Apparently, it was his staff who screwed up so he's trying to hang you, Parker, and my men to distract the media from it."

"Sonuvabitch," JW breathed, his torso falling back against the half-raised mattress.

"And the men who were evac'd from the ambush site?"

"Yeah?" JW nodded, wary.

"They're trying to court-martial them? They had nothing to do with it."

"They were taken to a medic camp. All but four were evac'd. The last four needed a couple more days before they were stable enough travel." Ben's dark eyes seemed almost black. "The camp was hit. The two-star's staff had told everyone it was empty. A lieutenant was in the comms tent and got word out."

His blood froze. *Talk about your big-ass cover-ups and fuck-ups!*

"How many…" JW swallowed. "How bad?"

"The lieutenant was determined to protect my men. The five of them and a couple others were the only survivors."

"Holy shit." Closing his eyes, JW shuddered. "That LT needs the highest medal we can give him."

"Her," Ben corrected. Eyes opening, JW stared at him as the Bostonian nodded. "You recall a two-star you shot on 9/11?"

"Yeah, Carruthers, from somewhere west."

"South Dakota," Ben supplied. "His men came to the rescue as the lieutenant got a sword through her shoulder."

"Holy shit," JW breathed, his mind spinning. "How bad?"

"Pretty bad. Stevens said there's no way the four of them would have survived without her. Get this – her father's a two-star and her brother is a major who's on the staff of a one-star. But that just added to the post-political brouhaha. So, to sum up, we have a two-star and his staff and *their* connections arguing with a two-star, his staff, and *their* connections."

JW shot him a baleful look.

"And all because you didn't want to work in an office."

"Backatacha," Ben grinned. "Not to worry, though. Our families have waded into the fray as well."

Considering that, JW fought back the grin.

"How many scalps do our grandmothers have?"

"Um, not our grandmothers," Ben cleared his throat and called behind him. "Ma'am?"

There was a quick double rap on the doorframe as Zoey came in. JW stared at her determined expression. *Ben's mother died years ago, but my mom? God knows she'd fight a brigade or two and take no prisoners. She'll have called in every political and business favor the family has and play every damn single one of them. The Pentagon doesn't stand a fucking chance.* Grinning, he turned his head to look at Ben.

"Good point. How many bodies have our cousins had to hide because of my mother?"

"Who said there was anything big enough left to bury?" his mother replied smoothly. "Sit down, Ben, before you fall down."

Sitting down in a bedside chair, Ben grinned as he bent over for his crutches.

"Oh, yeah. Brian and Bron were in the room taking notes. Between your mom and our grandmothers chiming in when Zoey stopped for a breath Brian said there wasn't enough for DNA testing. Last I heard it, the body count stands at five four-stars, four three-stars, six brigadiers, and a few colonels for good measure. People in the Pentagon run for the exits when they hear the name Zoey Franklin."

"Damn straight," Zoey nodded, going to Ben and kissing the top of his head before moving to her son and, without batting an eyelash, and stepping onto the side rail to kiss his cheek. "Mess with my boys." She snorted. "Idiots."

JW felt his heart burst with emotion.

"I love you, Mom."

"I love you more."

"Couldn't one of the two of them have smuggled a camera in there? Or a tape recorder? So we could hear what actually went down?" JW wondered, wistfully.

He'd heard from Grant a bit of how his mother acted in the board room when someone was an idiot. He could just imagine her facing down some of the senior officers in the entire country. *I've always known she would do anything, fight anyone for me. Really never thought she would actually take on the entire military hierarchy. I shouldn't be surprised though.*

Stepping away as he spoke, Zoey rolled her eyes and put her oversize bag on the floor next to Ben's chair. JW felt her gaze on him and turned from teasing Ben to look at her and felt his heart seize up. Under the sheets, where there should have been two long ridges where his legs were, the one on the right stopped halfway.

"Oh, my God," he breathed as images flashed through his mind and blackness threatened. Fighting back the panic, he stretched his hand toward his leg, then to her. The terror started to win. "Mom? Mom!"

In a heartbeat, she was up on the mattress, sitting down and wrapping her arms around him as tightly as she could. JW fought the shock, the pain that had been, and his eyes sought Ben's struggling expression, seeing the regret and grief that his friend had been so seriously injured in rescuing him from a hellish death.

"Ben, get the doctor. Ben," Zoey said sharply, causing the captain to snap to attention. "Get the doctor. Now."

"Yes, ma'am." Without hesitation, he got to his feet, tucked the crutches in his armpits, and hobbled to the door. Glancing over his shoulder as he opened it, he clenched his jaw as the man he'd admired since childhood wept in his mother's arms.

Chapter Seven

"You sure about this?" David wondered from the door as Ally packed.

"That's the tenth time you've asked that," Diana told him, coming from the closet with an armful of dresses.

"Twelfth," Ally laughed as her cousin-in-law placed the clothes in the hanging garment bag. "But who's counting?"

"You obviously," David drawled. "What did I do in previous lives to get two smart-ass women in my life at the same time?"

"Something absolutely amazing," his wife assured him, zipping up the bag and going to him.

Ally focused on folding the sweaters as the couple kissed.

Unable to get through a scene without using her safe word within fifteen minutes, she had finally suggested to Master Liam that she leave the Shadows. She was more than willing to return for demonstrations if she was needed, but it was time for her to face the rest of the world. To use what she'd learned about herself and get stronger.

David had automatically assumed she'd move back into their Long Island house. He and Diana had decided it was preferable to the penthouse for raising Matt and any additional children. Ally wanted to spread her wings though, and since they weren't going to live in the city, she figured she would live in the penthouse and see if she liked it. Carla, the housekeeper, was excited as it would be closer to Marcus's school. Marcus was excited because Ally treated him like the younger brother she'd never had. The ten-year-old was already planning weekend trips to museums and parks.

Ally was hoping she'd be busy enough to keep her mind distracted. What she heard from David about JW's injuries broke her heart. He'd lost the lower half of his right leg. She was desperate to see him but had no idea how to broach a visit with anyone or even who to speak with. David might seem the logical person to arrange a visit, but how was she to explain what JW meant to her? She wasn't sure and she certainly had no idea if she meant anything to him. And trying to tell her absurdly protective cousin when it came to *her* sex life that JW had picked her from the selection room? Yeah, she could just imagine that conversation..

Going to JW's mother was the next logical person, or even Gisele who had forgiven her for suddenly disappearing for months, but trying to explain why she would want to see him when, to their knowledge, they'd only met briefly at the party over a year ago just seemed more embarrassing than Ally could imagine.

Remembering Liam's advice to find her own strength so she could be strong for others, she was determined she would do just that. Then, maybe she'd be strong enough for JW. It had been one year since she'd been seduced by Kevin and, looking back, she was rather proud of her recovery from that nightmarish six weeks as well as her grief.

Now, closing the suitcase and zipping up the last garment bag, she set her shoulders. The grief of losing her family would always be with Ally, but they had loved her and that would also be with her. Whenever she joined them in heaven, she wanted them to be proud of her, of how she'd lived her life. She absolutely did not want to disappoint them. Or herself.

****

Gritting his teeth, JW put the prosthesis on, ignoring the medic's blather about how it would feel perfectly natural with practice, that he just needed to give it some time and other shit JW just wasn't feeling.

Exasperated, he paused and looked at the man. That his mother stayed quiet from her chair in the corner of the room told him she too was fed up with the nonsense and was waiting for him to "let it rip."

"Mister, how about we fucking blow up your life, cut off part of your leg and then, to put the final screws into the salt being rubbed into your wounds, threaten you with court-martial?" he growled, doing his damndest to sound as pissed off as he felt.

The medic stiffened at the tone and words, blinking as if he didn't have the slightest clue what JW was talking about.

"Get the fuck outta here," JW snarled, gesturing at the door. The man just stared at him. "Get out!"

To emphasize her son's words, Zoey went to the door and opened it, glaring at the medic until he stuttered and stumbled his way out.

"God, he sounded like Grandmother there for a minute," JW muttered, yanking at the straps.

Closing the door, Zoey returned to her chair and quietly watched him.

"Not anymore," she finally spoke. "Nearly losing her oldest grandson and having him wounded in a heroic act has lit a fire in her nearly as bright as in me."

Frowning he glanced at her.

"What do you mean?"

"She and Mrs. Hancock are now waging war against the Pentagon," Zoey told him, glee in her voice and dancing eyes. "They are using every trick ever invented and creating a few just for vengeful grandmothers." He could only stare at her and she laughed, shaking her head. "That's why I'm able to spend so much time with you, sweetheart. Those two are going at it so well that I'm just window dressing. I figure the top dog, JC something or other…" She tilted her head for him to fill in the blanks for her.

"JCS," he supplied, slightly dazed as he realized just what they'd been doing and who they'd been talking to. "The chairman of the Joint Chiefs of Staff. A four-star general. He's kind of a big deal in the military."

Zoey snorted and laughed.

"Well, by the time those two are done with him and everyone on their way up to him, they probably all felt like they were back in basic training getting yelled at for how they made their bed or how their shoes looked."

The image presented did what he hadn't been able to since he'd realized half his leg was gone. He tried to hold it back, pressing his lips together. The image of several men in uniform, stars twinkling from each shoulder, getting a dressing down from his grandmother and the equally redoubtable Mrs. Hancock as they were made to remake their beds or polish their boots finally got to him and he burst out laughing.

Just when he thought he had himself under control again, his glance landed on his mother. Her humor danced in her eyes and they'd both started laughing again.

Finally, he took a deep breath. His mother wiped her eyes and put a hand on her ribs.

"I haven't laughed like that in over a year," she whispered.

"Same here," he nodded. "Mom—" he stopped, not knowing what to say.

"Sh, sweetie," came her murmur as her hand covered his. "I want you to be quiet and listen to me. *Ben* is alive because you, Parker, and his men did what was right. What few other men would have done. Eh," she cut off his attempt to protest with a shake of her blonde head. "Shush. You knew that, if by some miracle you got to him in time, it would take another miracle for you to get him out safely. But that's all you thought of. All you focused on, right? Getting to Ben before they could murder him." JW nodded, rocking his upper body as he fought back the terror that they wouldn't make it. "None of the rest mattered. None of you probably considered what the military would do to you, because you didn't think you'd survive. But even knowing it was practically suicide to go after him, you did it anyway. You did what was right and honorable." She took a deep breath and he couldn't look away from her face. "Yes, you lost your lower right leg. And others were injured. But, I know damn well, if you'd known what the cost would be, you would have all gone anyway, right?"

"Yes," JW answered without hesitation. "We couldn't wait. We knew we had to go and get him."

"And do you really think that your family, that Ben's family, wouldn't understand that? That we would let anyone besmirch or belittle what you did, what you risked?" Her green eyes latched onto his face and he couldn't look away. He couldn't believe how fiercely he felt love pouring out of her. "Forget hell hath no fury like a woman scorned, son. Hell hath no fury like a grandmother protecting her grandchild and *that* is what *I* unleashed on the Pentagon."

"Zoey Franklin's personal WMD," he remarked. "Or would it be GMD? Grandmothers of Mass Destruction?"

His mother blinked then giggled.

"She'll like that. She and Mrs. Hancock will be by this afternoon after laying siege again."

"Then I better have made some progress to show them their efforts are appreciated," he decided aloud, finishing the last strap around his upper thigh. He stood, holding onto the back of the chair as he tried to get his balance. "I want to make you and them proud of me."

Zoey rose by his side and put his left arm around her shoulders.

"Son, if we were any prouder of you and the rest of them, we'd be exploding like nonstop fireworks."

"Well, how about helping me to the bathroom before my bladder explodes?" he suggested. "Just as an alternative."

"Excellent idea," she laughed. "You move and balance on me."

It took longer than he would have liked, but mostly because his mother let him determine the pace. Reaching the bathroom door to his room, he looked down at her.

"You're really wishing I was like five or six, had that sprained ankle, and you could carry me to the bathroom, don't you?"

"Yeah, I do," she confirmed. "It was easier to protect you then. Take care of you. Well, okay, you called it babying, but whatever." As he laughed, she slipped from under his arm. "Call for me after you're decent again."

"Yes, ma'am."

With his mother trying not to hover, JW decided to use the crutches to get to the therapy room he'd been assigned.

"Upper body workout," he called it as they left the room.

She walked at his side and gave him a sideways glance. "You'll want to hit me with a crutch if I say what I'm thinking."

"I can't imagine even thinking such a thing," he protested.

"Yeah, right," she drawled.

"What are you thinking?"

Yeah, this is Mom and there's no telling what she'll come up with.

"Well, because you're on crutches you're slower and I can actually walk at my normal pace instead of racing to *try* and keep up with you, which, by the way, I've been doing since you took your first step."

"Mom." He said with a sigh.

"Yes, dear?"

"I'm thinking it."

Laughing, she reached out and opened the door for the therapy room.

Hours later, as he was dripping with sweat, the sadist lieutenant also known as his therapist finally let him sit down next to his fidgeting mother.

"I'm all right, Mom," he murmured. "The woman knew what she was doing and that she had to push me like that."

"I don't give a shit," she muttered back, eyeing the younger woman who stood twenty feet away with her next patient. "I didn't like her talking to you like that."

"If you were doing it, you'd have been saying the same damn things to me." JW bit back the grin. *God, she is the best.*

"That's totally different," she retorted.

"How so?" he asked, even though he was pretty sure of her answer.

"I'm your mother. I'm allowed to say those things to you."

He laughed before resting his head on her shoulder.

"God, how did I manage to get you for a mother?"

"God is testing me for something," she said drily.

"Testing, rewarding, or punishing?" he quipped.

"Yes."

They laughed at themselves as the nearest door in the gymnasium-size room opened. Seeing his grandmother and Mrs. Hancock, the manners drummed into his head from childhood came to the fore and JW struggled to his feet. Henrietta hurried forward and embraced him. Putting his arms around her, he tried to hide his shock. There were tears in her eyes. He'd seen his grandmother cry about as often as his mother or grandfather.

"Oh, my sweet boy," she murmured, framing his face with her hands the way she did when he was a boy trying to get out of trouble, which, he admitted, had been enough to give her most if not all of her gray hair. "My brave sweet boy." She turned to the woman with her. "What do you think of our boy, Alma?"

"Words cannot express what I'm thinking or feeling right now," Alma Hancock told her, joining her to embrace him. "You saved Ben. You and the other men. Words have not been invented to express the emotions the Hancocks are feeling."

"Thank you, ma'am," he murmured, now completely out of sorts with the two women who were usually so stoic.

"Sit, sit," his grandmother urged. "Since your mother let us play in the Pentagon," Henrietta winked—*winked*—JW nearly fell into the chair, at her daughter who grinned up at her. "Unsupervised. We have some stories to tell."

An alert corporal arrived with two plastic chairs.

"Thank you, young man," they murmured, settling themselves as regally as if on hand-carved thrones.

"Tell them what you dubbed them," Zoey told her son.

"Zoey Franklin's GMD," he responded. "Grandmothers of Mass Destruction."

The two women, both in their late seventies, blinked then roared with laughter. Henrietta hugged her daughter.

"The Pentagon probably wishes that's all we were," Alma applauded, glancing as a far door opened. "Ah, there they all are."

JW's jaw dropped as Ben, Parker, and the rest of nine men walked over. He stood and saluted Ben, who solemnly returned the gesture then hugged his grandmother.

"I didn't hear reports of mass casualties," Ben observed. "So, I guess you just took prisoners?"

The two women beamed smugly at each other.

"I think that's how we looked that one time," JW muttered to Ben.

"Which time?" Ben wondered.

"In or out of uniform?" JW queried.

"Yeah, we came by it honestly, didn't we?" Ben grinned at Alma.

"And no bail necessary," JW added.

"For these two, can you imagine what it would be?" Zoey wondered, flashing a grin at her mother.

JW couldn't believe the grin on his grandmother's face.

"I think we could manage to break them out," Ben mused. "Quincy? Do you think you can hack into a prison system?"

"To break out Mrs. Hancock and Mrs. Franklin? And Miss Zoey? Absolutely," the tall somber looking Sioux sergeant replied with a slight twinkle in his dark eyes. "The rest of you? Not a blipping chance."

"Yeah, well, that we expected," Corporal Watson joked.

"Oh, yeah," another chuckled.

"We're all here, Grannie," Ben said quietly. "Did they make a decision?"

Alma Hancock straightened her already-perfect posture and looked each man in the eye. JW felt his mother's fingers tighten on his.

"The Pentagon has finally seen sense," she told them. "No charges will be brought against any of you for disobeying orders or anything else. And," she replied as sighs of relief whooshed through them, "you are all being put in for various commendations and awards. I lost track of what he was saying at that point. Did you understand any of it, Henrietta?"

"Not much," she admitted. "I told him to just put all of you in for the highest and that *might* be sufficient. He said they would do everything possible." She smirked at Alma, who grinned back at her. "If only to make sure we don't enter that building again."

"I'll be damned," JW breathed, stunned.

"Well, not yet at least," his mother sighed, smiling up at him. "Not yet."

At the knock on his door, JW glanced up from the book his mother had brought him that morning. Seeing the man coming in, he chuckled and waved the paperback.

"Cool. Sign it, will you?"

"Abso-fucking-lutely," Boone Hancock grinned, putting the briefcase on the swivel table and flipping the catches. Pulling out a pen, he cringed as JW folded a corner to mark his spot. "Good God, man. That's not how you treat a book."

"I don't want to lose my place," JW pointed out, handing him the book. "The villain just killed the third woman."

"Ah," Boone murmured, taking a paper bookmark from the case, inserting it and

smoothing out the corner. "The body count gets higher."

"Not all his I hope," JW prompted for a hint as Boone scribbled on the front page.

"Oh, no," came the wink. "The hero is almost an antihero."

"I've noticed he has a dark side."

JW took the book and read the inscription. *To JW, a hard-ass hero. And inspiration for a new series. Boone.* Stunned, he turned his head to stare at the writer. Four years younger, Boone had rougher edges than the rest of the Hancocks, as his father had run away when he was eighteen. JW wasn't quite sure how Boone had spent his early years, but was pretty sure they'd been a helluva lot harder than anything he'd gone through as the illegitimate son of Zoey Franklin. It was in the other man's eyes and reflexes. Now, Boone returned his gaze steadily, aware and ready for questions. To a point. JW wouldn't cross the unspoken line and Boone knew it.

"Inspiration? Boone, what the hell?" he wondered.

"Well, you, Ben, and the rest," Boone answered. "I've already outlined the first three books and sent them to my agent. My current publisher is scrambling to outbid everyone else who, naturally," he grinned, "are throwing out very nice offers."

"So, if I need a loan?" JW grinned.

"I was thinking a mortgage," Boone drawled, taking a folder from the case and handing it over. "Although, I doubt you would need one."

Putting the manila file on his thighs, JW opened it and frowned at the top page—a photograph of a cabin in a meadow, trees behind it, and an established path leading through it. He read the description: three bedrooms, three baths, master suite on ground floor, garage with studio apartment. Basement family room with its own fireplace, large root cellar. Remodeled kitchen. Plumbing, wiring, and roof updated in 1999. Established fruit trees and well-cared for garden.

"Boone, what is this?"

Well, beyond the obvious. Fortunately Boone understood what he meant.

"My neighbor's," he replied. "He's a WWII and Korea veteran. His wife died of cancer this past summer, and he's decided he doesn't want to be around so many memories. Or deal with another winter. He mentioned it to me last week. I asked him not to put it on the market until I talked to you."

"Me?" JW shook his head, even as he read the next page with details on the twenty acres. The path went to the lake with a dock and small boat house. No motorboats were allowed. "Boone, I live—"

"Wherever the Army has sent you," Boone nodded. "After being on your own so long, do you really want to move back into the family house on Long Island?"

Snapping his jaw shut, JW considered that. It was probably exactly what his mother and the rest of the family expected. God knew, it was what his mother would want after nearly losing him. And it would drive him crazy in a week. *But a cabin in the Connecticut woods?* He'd visited Boone a couple years earlier, soon after the man's first book had hit the bestseller lists. While only a couple hours from New York City, it had been worlds apart. Quiet. Peaceful. Woods. Lake. His gaze went to the photos.

"You wouldn't be coming over every day to borrow sugar or anything, would you?" JW gave him a sideways glance.

"Nah," Boone shook his head with a smirk. "I'm sweet enough as it is."

JW snorted at that.

"My mother and grandmother will go apeshit," he murmured. "Um."

Narrowed eyes lasered on the man who suddenly wouldn't look at him.

"You told them about this before showing me?" JW demanded.

"This morning as we all met for breakfast in the hotel dining room, they were talking about redecorating your suite before you went home. My grandmother was chiming in."

"Oh, lord," JW groaned. "Last time Grandmother did that was when I left for basic. She might have meant well, but I did not appreciate all the olive-drab green paint when I came home at Christmas."

"Exactly. I figured that might happen so I told Bron and Grant last night," Boone explained. "They'll be by after their meeting by the way." JW nodded. "And Grant actually brought it up at breakfast."

"Grant?" *Was he trying to make sure I didn't up and decide to take my place in the company?*

"Yup. He pointed out that you'd been on your own for fifteen years, and no grown man of thirty-three was going to want to move back home."

"I'll bet that went down well since Grandmother brow-beat all four of her children into staying in the mansion. Minus their 'vacation homes'," JW commented. His mother staying, he got, but he still couldn't figure out how the matriarch had managed to keep them all there. No one ever talked about it.

"Exactly, but I think Grant sees you moving out as a way for him and Bron to break free as well. He also added that you'd only be a couple hours away." Boone chuckled. "So, he could still loop you into board meetings if he needed your particular skill set."

JW had to laugh at that.

"And Mom and Grandmother accepted that?"

"It took some more talking, and I'm still not sure if they fully accepted it. Your mother was fussing," Boone admitted, grimacing. "Your grandmother said something about an early Christmas present so you could get around. You know what that means?"

Considering that, JW smiled slowly.

"My truck is sixteen years old. I think I'll give it to Nick. Just to wind her up a bit. I think she'll appreciate it."

Laughing, Boone pulled out his cell phone.

"So, you want it?"

"Hell, yes. And you knew I would."

Smirking, Boone tapped out the numbers. Settling back on the pillows, JW reviewed the information and the photographs.

"I'll keep the furnishings," he commented as Boone talked to the owner. His eyes flicked over as Boone nodded. "Whatever he doesn't want to take. God knows I've got nothing of my own."

"Nah, you're just a poor soul without a cent to his name," came the observation from the door.

Grinning, JW watched Grant and Bron stride in. Bron took the plastic chair to JW's right while Grant leaned on the metal railing at the foot of the bed.

"I was wondering if family was going to come see me," he drawled, gesturing at Boone who smirked at the pair. "I've seen more Hancocks than I have Franklins."

"Does Aunt Zoey not count as family?" Bron wondered, raising an eyebrow. "I could tell her that she can check out of the hotel and go home."

"Like hell you will," JW snorted. "And she wouldn't even if you did."

There were a few things he was certain of and his mother staying near him until he could leave the hospital was an absolute.

"We had some business to sort through," Grant said by way of apology, then jerked a thumb at Bron. "And he was helping Ben with some sort of legal crap."

"I thought that was all settled." Frowning, JW put the property paperwork down on the folder. "What's happened now?"

"Well, he and his men realized nearly being court-martialed wasn't an encouragement to stay in the military, so Ben decided to start his own business," Bron answered. "He's setting up a security-slash-investigative company and hiring all the men who came after him. He's already leased a suite in Keith's building."

"Keith's building?" JW raised a hand to slow him down. "Back up a minute."

"Keith's eccentric great-uncle, the one who refused to have anything to do with the family company when Keith's father took over," Bron filled in. JW nodded. "Well, he went into real estate. Maybe not as extensively as Trump, but he got some prime spots and did well. He died in April and left everything to Keith." Bron chuckled. "Probably to piss off everyone else, which it did. His father and uncles tried to contest the will, but it was pretty ironclad. So, the MacLauren building is now Keith's, along with the rest. First thing he did was start renovating the top twelve floors for residences. The second to fourth floors are being renovated for shops and cafes or whatever small businesses he can get. He's hired Charles O'Leary to head up a security division and then he" Bron smiled. "He's offering reduced rents for those who were in the impact area of the Towers."

"Nice," JW approved.

"And," Grant picked up the story, "The residences are being fitted with, well, he's calling them panic rooms." A knowing smile appeared on his face. "But they can also be used for other purposes."

All four men in the room had the same sexual proclivities and grinned.

"So, you two have apartments there? Or will? Grandmother's going to think we're all deserting her," he commented, recalling that his mother had commented on her brothers and their wives trying to spend as much time traveling as possible the past several years.

"Gisele is still at the big house," Grant reminded him. "Although if she's not studying, she's spending a lot of time with David's cousin. What's her name?" Grant glanced at Bron. "The one who married Kevin?"

"Ally," Bron reminded him.

"Gisele seems calmer around Ally, so that's a good thing." The brown eyes rolled at his younger sister's behavior. Grant held their grandmother's opinion on the O'Grady blood. "At least we're not having to deal with as many of her 'episodes'."

"Back off," JW growled, as much for the insinuation about the O'Grady inheritance as for the mention of Ally, especially the reference of her marriage.

"Yeah, whatever," Bron shrugged. "Grandmother approves so that helps Gisele."

"That's good. What else has been going on with the group? I got a note from Brody to get home for a game."

"The New York group has been managing," answered Grant. "Brody's worked his way into the office next to his father. His sister Rose spends as much time at the grandparents' as she does at her own home. You knew about the mountain climbing accident that killed their father's cousin and wife, right?"

"Nope," JW shook his head as Boone ended his call. "Wait a second. I remember he mentioned relatives always gallivanting about the globe."

"That's the one," confirmed Grant. "They had a daughter they never saw. She was in a boarding school somewhere in Europe. Brody's parents brought her back home. She's a couple years younger than Rose and Heather." He glanced at Bron. "I forget anything?"

"Keith's company," was the answer.

"Like the buildings he inherited isn't enough to keep him busy?" JW blinked in surprise. "There had to have been a dozen or so in Manhattan alone."

"About that," Grant nodded. "He started up a software company in late July, saying California shouldn't have a monopoly on it. MacLauren Computing takes up two floors of the building."

"Damn." JW was impressed. "How's he doing?"

"Pretty good as far as I can tell. He underbid and won a couple city contracts and brought them in early so he's getting a good reputation." Grant frowned. "Something happened with his family over the Fourth of July."

"Shit. What was it?" JW frowned, recalling Keith had never gotten along well with any family member. After he'd started college, things had gone from bad to icy.

Grant shook his head.

"Not sure. He absolutely refuses to discuss it, but he's back in contact with his mother."

JW stared at him. "You're serious? His mother? The one who up and left him without even a good-bye when he was six?"

"That's the one," confirmed Grant. "I'm not sure what happened, but he's pretty much completely broken off from his father's family."

"Wow," JW marveled at that, then glanced at Boone. "How's your family? Although I think I've seen most of them the past few weeks."

"Boston's been quiet compared to New York," he grinned. "Besides a parade or two," he threw in the taunt. The three New Yorkers glared at him. "Brian's like Grant—determined to run the company without a hovering elder before he's thirty. Sam is still in school with Nick, and those two are thick as thieves. Sarah, Louisa, and Josie are trying to convince their individual parents and our grandparents to let them move to London or Paris for a year."

"How's that going?" JW wondered, imagining how his grandfather would react after his mother's semester abroad.

"Grandmother is actually all for it," Boone grinned. "Grandfather is having palpitations at the thought of his granddaughters leaving the nest. I figure by Christmas they'll have worn him down. And he'll end up buying them a castle or something he can put a moat and barbwire around."

The four chuckled. JW tapped the papers on his lap.

"And the cabin?"

"There's no moat," Boone replied with a straight face. "Just the lake."

"Smart-ass," muttered JW. "What did he say?"

"He's faxing the paperwork to the hotel. Bron can go over it—"

"I don't know real estate law," came the protest.

"Improvise," JW shot back. "You're fairly intelligent or so I've been told."

"Is this what I have to look forward to?" Bron complained. "Being the unpaid legal expert for family and friends?"

"Yeah, pretty much," JW confirmed with a smirk.

"We'll keep your liquor cabinet filled," Grant offered.

"With the best," warned Bron, wagging a finger at him. "Only top shelf."

"Of course," grinned his cousins.

Chapter Eight

Ally couldn't believe what she was doing. She'd tried everything she could to get out of it, but David had countered her every argument. He'd finally played the family card, saying he'd never had anyone on his side in a meeting like this. Everyone else in the room would have family with them and, for once, he wanted to know what it felt like. Now, he could have his wife and a cousin. Put like that, further arguments would have just sounded churlish and childish. And while she would always be grateful for what he and Diana had done for her the past year, Ally finally felt stronger, more confident in dealing with people in David's business circles. Certainly after the last board meeting, David had been impressed. He hadn't said anything in front of the other members, but once the door between the conference room and his office had closed, he had whooped and spun her around.

And, as the taxi worked its way through traffic, Ally had to admit the real reason she'd been trying to get out of it. The Franklins would be there. She didn't know how many or who and was very afraid that JW would be there. *How am I supposed to act natural around him? How am I supposed to not run to him, ask if he's all right, and beg him to touch me? Anywhere, anyway he wants?*

"Oh, God, I can't believe I let him talk me into this," she groaned, letting her head fall back and staring at the ceiling.

"What was that, miss?" the taxi driver wondered.

"Nothing," she replied, lifting her head and smiling. "I was wondering how I let my cousin talk me into this meeting."

"Ah," he nodded understanding. "For family, we will do the most ridiculous things. For those we love, we will do the most dangerous and not count the cost for either."

"That is so very true," she agreed with the profoundness of his statement.

"And here you are, miss," he announced, stopping directly in front of the doorman for the address David had given her.

She gave him the fare and a generous tip as the door was open.

"Are you expected, miss?" the doorman inquired, escorting her in as another took his place.

"I am," she replied, realizing they weren't just doormen but security. "Miss Brown. Twentieth floor. A meeting with the Franklins."

The man behind the desk, who was definitely bulked up like a security guard, frowned. A second guard glanced at a list as if searching for anyone expected by the Franklins.

"Which Franklin?"

"I have no idea," she replied, shaking her head.

All three men scowled at her. *Damn it, David, you had to know I'd need that information.*

"Miss Brown, I'm sorry but I don't see your name on the list and if you don't know who you're meeting then—"

Behind the guard desk, a door opened as she prepared to damn her cousin again, and a tall man entered the lobby. Eyes the color of leaves in spring lasered in on her. She drank him in with a single look—black leather coat over a black sweater that clung to his thick chest and faded blue jeans. His chiseled features were paler than when she'd last seen him, indicating how he'd had to spend so much time indoor recuperating. She had to smile when she saw the combat boots along with the same brush military haircut. *You can take the soldier out of the Army, but you can't take the Army out of him.*

"Ally, what good timing," JW rumbled, striding to her without a hint of having lost part of his leg.

Stunned at the sight of him, she managed to nod as the guards around the desk practically snapped to attention.

"You know her, Mr. Franklin?" the one behind the desk inquired.

"Indeed. Please don't delay us further," JW advised, extending his hand out to her. "The meeting started a few minutes ago."

"Of course, sir," a guard replied.

At the buzz, she went through the turnstile. His hand went to her left elbow as they walked toward the bank of elevators beyond the guard desk. Silently, JW pushed the elevator call button. Struggling to control her breathing, to appear normal, she stood next to him in front of the crack in the doors.

"Good thing I took the stairs up from the garage level," he commented.

"What—" Ally could only stare at him. *He's so calm. As if he expected to see me and was ready to hide his emotions. Or he knew he'd see me and has no emotions for me.*

"We'll talk later," he murmured.

"Talk," she echoed. *Well, that could be good.*

"You want more?" JW asked in the same cool voice.

Feeling as if she'd been slapped, her head jerked around to see his inscrutable expression. Biting her lower lip, Ally resolutely faced the doors, praying they would open soon. The beep signaled its arrival and the doors separated. She took back the prayer with a terrified gasp. Even as she instinctively stumbled backward, the man at the front of the elevator grabbed her right forearm.

"What the hell are you doing here?" Kevin MacLauren demanded. "Are you stalking me? You pathetic little bitch!"

"I'm not stalking you!" she protested, twisting to get away from his painful grip.

"Get your fucking hands off of her," growled JW, a hand coming down and gripping Kevin's forearm. Ally glimpsed the guards moving quickly in their direction. "Hold the doors," he ordered as they started to slide together.

"Sir," came the answer inside the car with a prompt beep as the doors halted.

"Sir?" The nearest guard called out.

"I've got this," JW told him. "Stand down."

"Yes, sir."

Security took two steps back, staying alert and ready to back him up if he needed it. *David wasn't kidding when he said security here was tight.*

Not moving, Ally watched her ex-husband straightened and tried to look down his nose at the man by her side. JW stood with his feet planted about a foot apart. *If looks could kill, Kevin would be halfway to China.*

"Get your hands off of her," JW repeated.

"Who the hell are you to tell me what to do?" Kevin's voice chilled her soul and his fingers bit like steel into her flesh. Using every trick she'd learned in therapy and her own studies, she fought back the nightmare. *He can't hurt me anymore. Stay calm and you can get through this.* "This is private and none of your concern."

Her ex's arrogant, superior tone jolted her back to the present. Ally nearly rolled her eyes. That would get him nowhere with the master she knew. Without answering, JW tightened his fingers on Kevin's wrist like a vise. Ally watched in satisfaction as JW's knuckles turned white and pain filled her ex's face. With a gasp, he released her arm.

"Are you all right?" JW asked her.

"I'm fine," she replied, managing to smile up at him.

"I don't know who the hell you are, but when I get to my meeting, I will be sure to have you removed—"

As he spoke, her ex stepped back into the elevator and nearly choked when JW pulled her into the car.

"What are you doing?" he demanded hotly.

"Let's go," JW told the liveried man.

As the elevator operator released the door open button, JW's arm held her tightly against his side. JW raised an eyebrow as his gaze went from her to the nearly apoplectic man on the other side of the car. Ally looked at Kevin's anger-flushed face and wondered if he was going to have a heart attack.

"Fools," muttered her ex, straightening his coat and smoothing back his hair. "Follow me. You will rue the day you pissed me off."

Ally clapped a hand over her mouth and unsuccessfully smothered a giggle. Her ex was arrogant enough to assume that they'd just blindly follow him.

"You dumb bitch!" he snarled, taking a step toward her.

JW stiff-armed him.

"Touch her again and I'll toss you out the nearest window."

"Are you threatening me?" Kevin's eyes widened in shock.

"Threats are a waste of time. That was a promise." JW grinned with obvious malice at the smaller man.

"No one threatens me and gets away with it."

If possible, Kevin seemed to puff up even more with his growing ire. The elevator came to a stop and the doors opened. The operator stared pointedly at Kevin.

"Your floor, sir."

Her ex strode out and disappeared down the hall.

JW stepped out, bringing Ally with him. Pulling her to the left where several ficus trees created an alcove, he held her against his chest. For a brief moment, she closed her eyes, feeling herself calm down after the violent encounter, and drew strength from him. His hands stroked up and down her back. One cupped her ass, while the other caressed the back of her neck.

"Ally. Look at me."

Hearing the rasp in his voice, Ally was shocked by his cock hardening and pressing against her stomach. She lifted her head and met his gaze.

"Yes, sir?"

Amusement twinkled briefly in his eyes at her automatic response. His hand squeezed her ass and her pussy tightened in response. She had to remind herself that she absolutely would not drop to her knees and pull his cock out. No matter how much she wanted to suck him deep into her throat. She would not beg him to fuck her.

His lips brushed her ear and the low growl of his voice nearly made her come right then and there.

"You're coming with me…"

"No, I can't," she gasped. "I have to…"

His tongue clicked against his teeth and she winced at the soft reproach. Last time she'd heard him react like that, he'd spanked her, before fucking her ass. The last time he'd fucked her. Ally fought back the moan of need. *Dammit. What is it about this man that he affects me like this when no one else can?*

JW gazed down at her.

"I can see it in your eyes, Ally. I know exactly what you want me to do." Heat flared in his eyes. "And that you're fighting the urge to kneel in front of me, aren't you?" His voice dropped and she nodded.

"Yes, sir," she whispered. She'd missed him, yes, but... "But..."

"You're staying by my side during this meeting and then leaving with me," he told her. The vibrations of his voice in her ear had her entire body trembling. His hands pressed her against his chest and her breath caught in her throat. His cock was fully erect. "Any argument?"

"N...no, sir," she stammered.

She didn't care where they went. He was here. He wanted her with him. He wanted *her*. She had this effect on him. She nearly cheered.

"Good girl."

He took her hand and drew her down the hall. Opening one-half of the double doors at the end of the hall, JW pulled Ally into a conference room. Several people gathered in two main groups at the ends of the table. David and Diana sat in the middle, closer to the Franklin side. Grant glanced over at them.

"I was wondering if you had decided not to join us," he said blandly.

"Kevin MacLauren assaulted Miss Brown in the elevator," JW replied, adroitly moving her so he stood between her and the MacLauren end of the table.

Kevin sneered.

"Are you so paranoid, David, that you hire a bodyguard for her? She's hardly worth any ransom." He sniffed and Ally's hard-won confidence slipped a couple notches. "Honestly, I don't know why you haven't packed her off back to Maine where she belongs."

Seeing Diana bristle, Ally rallied. As entertaining as it would have been to see the English aristocrat take Kevin down a few pegs, she knew she had to do it. His hand at her right elbow, JW guided her to a seat two down from Bronson. Glancing up at JW, she saw his eyes narrowed when he glanced at Kevin. *Better do something fast or this could go from bad to worse.*

"After some of my experiences with the so-called *gentlemen* of New York City, trust me," she drawled, "I'd much rather deal with a Maine lobster trap."

"Back up a minute," David was scowling. "He assaulted Ally?"

"Grabbed her arm," JW replied, taking the chair to her right, placing himself between her and the MacLaurens.

"I'll probably have bruises," she murmured, reflexively rubbing where his fingers had gripped her. *Focus, focus, focus. The MacLaurens are glaring at David and Diana, clearly not happy to see them.* Her eyes shifted to the folder—*South Pacific Ventures*—gold lettering gleamed on the stiff blue cover. *Bingo.*

"God dammit," her cousin growled as his wife caught his arm to keep him from rising.

"David." Ally caught her cousin's eye, smiling slightly. He froze, gave her an "all right, do it" look and settled back in his seat. "Tell me, Alan," she addressed her former father-in-law. "Are you still trying to develop that land in the South Pacific? On Sumatra, wasn't it? I would have thought if it was such a perfect spot you would have had people trampling each other to partner you on it." Dark eyes narrowed as her ex shifted in his seat. "Perhaps it's not such prime real estate after all. I mean, if Kevin felt the only way to get someone to agree to the deal was to marry me…"

"Wasted effort," Kevin muttered.

"Fortunately, since you decided to annul the marriage, I can *legally* say the nightmare never happened," she smiled sweetly at him. "Perhaps one day, you'll find a woman who accepts responsibility for all your daily challenges like traffic, bad coffee, and five-second erections."

Kevin roared in anger and surged to his feet. His two youngest half-brothers held him as they glanced at the other end of table. The Franklins struggled not laugh. Bronson finally gave in even as he tried to cover it with a cough.

JW fought to hold his temper in check. *She's got some fire in her. Dammit, what did that asshole do to her in six weeks of marriage?*. It had been a near thing in the lobby. The terror in her eyes when MacLauren had grabbed her had sent a rare rage surging up his spine, leaving him ready to kill.

"I wouldn't do that if I were you," JW's deep voice rumbled.

Alan MacLauren sent him a scathing glance.

"Bodyguards are not included in this meeting. You can wait outside."

"I don't think so," he replied. There was an empty seat to his mother's right where she sat next to Grant. *Where she expected me to sit.* He caught her raised eyebrow and the twitch at the corner of her mouth. His grandfather and uncles managed bland expressions, although humor glinted in their eyes. From the opposite side of the table, two seats away from David, Giselle winked at him. *Thank God for families that catch on quickly.*

"Enough," Alan thundered. "Hal, what kind of meeting have you invited us to? That people who have no clue what they're talking about," he gestured at Ally, "are invited is bad enough. But to let the help actually sit down and—"

"It's absurd," muttered his brother. "As if he would have the slightest idea of our business."

"And it's not as if Ally has a brain cell," Kevin added, glowering at her. "Bad enough Brown brought his wife, but the Franklins have two women sitting at their end. As if they'll understand."

That last insult pushed the wrong button for the Franklin men. JW glimpsed his mother's eyes narrowing and remembered her letter and the comment about Kevin. *Yup, if she could curse someone, Kevin would be toast.* His grandfather had had enough.

"It must be so difficult living in the wrong century," Hal Franklin remarked in a hard voice.

"Well, honestly, Hal," protested the other patriarch. "Just who is in charge down there? Your grandfather writes a trust that allows women a seat on the board. And none of the men try to stop it. You basically turn the company over to a grandson who's practically an amateur. What the hell is that about?"

"Shut the fuck up, Alan. My apologies, ladies," Hal said quickly, his eyes moving swiftly to his daughter, granddaughter, Diana, and Ally. "This gentleman is not Ally's bodyguard. He is my oldest grandchild, JW Franklin."

"What?" Kevin gaped.

At Grant's right, Zoey smiled as sweetly as Ally had.

"My son."

"No fucking way should he be here," Kevin protested. "He's a cripple. He's not a real man—"

Both Ally and Zoey leapt to their feet, lips curled back in snarls.

"You son-of-a-bitch," growled Zoey, leaning over the table.

"You don't know what it takes to be a man," snarled Ally.

"Mom, Ally," JW murmured, putting a hand over Ally's fist and glancing down the table at his mother's furious expression.

He could see the effort they both put into recovering their control. Ally sat down first, glancing at the older woman. JW couldn't recall his mother ever being this angry at anyone.

"You get first crack," Ally suggested in a mild tone that deceived no one. "I saw a custodial closet down the hall. I'm sure I could find a broom and dustpan to clean up the mess."

Taking a deep breath, Zoey winked and sat down.

JW met Grant's questioning glance with a bland one of his own. *Why the hell would Ally be so pissed? Unless she hates Kevin so much she'll do anything to embarrass him in public.*

"Are all meetings this exciting?" he drawled.

"Thinking of attending more?" his cousin wondered, biting back a smile.

"Not hardly," he fired back, eyes roving around the table. "Family is one thing," his gaze landed on the MacLaurens, "I've had enough of dealing with enemies."

"You do have a particular skill set," Bron reminded him with a grin.

"Which I'm not allowed to use as a civilian or on a civilian," JW retorted.

"Could we get to the business at hand?" Alan MacLauren bristled, tapping the thick folder before him, which was similarly placed before everyone else. "This is a prime piece of real estate and studies have shown—"

"Are these the same studies done eighteen months ago?" Ally questioned in a bland tone as she opened the file in front of her. "Which tab shows those results?"

"Studies show that the tourism boards…" Alan continued as if she hadn't spoken.

"I'm sorry," Zoey lifted a finger, as her eyes searched the open folder before her, "but which tab was that? The studies aren't mentioned in the contents."

"The tourism boards of the countries in the South Pacific will be touting the island—"

"Which tab?" growled Jonas Franklin, still rankled by the jibe at his oldest child being an amateur.

"Oh, yes," Alan smiled at him. "Appendix B."

"When were they done?" Henry Franklin, Bronson's father, asked.

"Eighteen months ago," Alan replied coolly.

"Apparently a lack of manners is hereditary," observed Adam Franklin. "Did you not hear our sister's question? Or Ally's?"

Biting back a grin, JW leaned back in his chair. Whatever grief the Franklin brothers might have given their sister over a lifetime, they would not stand for people insulting her.

"I prefer not to respond to the babblings of sluts," Alan remarked, his sneering gaze going from Ally to Zoey. "Young or old."

JW shot out of his chair before anyone else could process the words. Striding down the table, he grabbed the older man by the lapels of his suit jacket and hauled him to his feet. Ally froze in shock as David and the Franklin men stood.

"You will apologize to my mother and Ally now or I will fucking throw you out that window," he snarled, nose-to-nose with the man. "And if I ever hear of you or another MacLauren even hinting of an insult toward them, you will deal with me. And trust me," he smiled viciously, "you don't want to deal with me."

"That's...that's a threat," Alan stuttered. "You've threatened me!"

"I didn't hear anything," Bronson remarked, glancing around the table. "Except JW wanting your apology to Aunt Zoey and Ally."

"Same thing I heard," Grant and David chimed in.

"What are you talking about?" Kevin demanded, getting to his feet and stabbing a finger in JW's direction. "He said the same thing to me in the elevator."

"After you threatened and assaulted me," Ally reminded him. He glared at her.

"You might actually need to hire a bodyguard."

JW simply reached out, caught the front of his shirt and hauled him over the table.

"Threatening your former wife?" he questioned, keeping his voice soft.

"I've had enough of your bullshit," a baritone growl came from across the table.

Ally looked at her cousin in surprise. *Diana's not going to hold him back this time.*

There was a quick double rap at the doors and the right one opened before anyone could respond or move. A tall, muscular man in a tailored business suit appeared, took in the tableau in a glance, and shook his head. Looking over her shoulder, Ally gave him a sympathetic glance. Keith had been the only one in Kevin's family she had liked, even if she'd only met him at a crowded Thanksgiving dinner. He'd mentioned something about starting a software company.

"I was worried I'd be too late to prevent any bloodshed," he commented.

"Morning, Keith," Grant greeted him. "Which end would you like to sit at?"

"Neither, thanks," Keith replied with a wry smile. "What did my father and half-brother say that irritated JW?"

"They insulted Aunt Zoey and Ally," Bron filled him in.

"Jesus," Keith groaned, briefly closing his eyes and shaking his head. "Thank God I got my brains from my mother and not the paternal side of the family."

"Your mother…" snarled Alan.

"Careful, Father," Keith responded with a thin smile. "Remember what happened last time you insulted my mother. And I don't have the training and experience JW does. Or would you like me to refresh your memory from the Fourth of July?"

With a last shake of both men, JW released them, dropping Kevin on the table and returned to his seat next to Ally. The rest of his family except Grant sat down. Kevin's younger brothers helped him off the mahogany table and into his seat.

"Franklins," Grant spoke firmly. "Based on the folder and the recent discussion, does anyone need more time to consider their decision?" Heads shook in the negative around the table. "I put it to a vote then. Grandfather, do we make this deal?"

"No," rumbled Hal.

"Aunt Zoey?"

"No," she said flatly.

"Dad? Uncle Henry? Uncle Adam?"

JW sent Grant a grin of appreciation for ensuring his mother's position was emphasized.

"No," all three brothers replied firmly.

"JW, Bron, and Giselle?"

"No," the cousins answered.

Smiling slightly, Grant aimed his cold blue eyes at the senior MacLauren.

"It's unanimous, Mr. MacLauren. The Franklin family does not wish to do business with yours. For many reasons and on many levels."

"This is outrageous," sputtered Kevin with indignation. "Did you even read the proposal?"

"Of course," Grant replied easily. "Last December when you first gave it to David."

Aware of undercurrents and tensions she didn't fully understand, Ally held herself very still. She'd picked up on the simmering loathing between the ends of the table. It was too deep to have developed in the last year over a failed business proposal to David. *One he apparently shared with Grant.*

Stepping away from the door, Keith pushed it open more.

"I suggest the MacLaurens leave my building before I notify O'Leary of the situation," he said quietly.

Ally surmised that O'Leary was head of building security. *His building? Was that new? Not that I spent more than an hour or so around him and we barely talked.* Catching the way Kevin and the younger half-brothers glared at Keith, she was suddenly very glad that JW was between her and them.

"Keith, you're siding against the family?" An uncle of Kevin's demanded.

Keith gave him a level look.

"I think that question was answered a while ago," he replied. "Or would you like a refresher as well?"

Pushing away from the table, Grant strode to the door. The Franklin men stood as if ready to go to his side if necessary. Out of the corner of her eye, Ally saw David stand as well. She and Diana locked eyes. *What the hell is going on?*

"Franklin Enterprises will not collaborate with MacLauren Corporation." Grant moved to the still open door and pulled it wider. "Please leave."

Muttering under their breaths, the older four MacLaurens stood and walked out, the younger brothers on their heels. Kevin started to follow then spun to glare at Ally.

"You haven't heard the last from me. You or your friends," Kevin warned.

"Is that supposed to frighten us?" Bronson taunted, moving to stand behind Ally's chair so Kevin couldn't flank JW.

"Maybe we'll rue the day?" JW murmured sarcastically.

Kevin swore and stalked out. For a long moment, no one moved or spoke, as if trying to process everything that had happened.

"Could someone please explain what that was all about?" Diana finally demanded as she surged to her feet.

"Please," Ally agreed with a nod as she stood.

"Long story," David told them.

"It would have been nice if you'd filled me in on that long story a year ago," Ally sniped. "Maybe before I married him?"

"I told you not to," he reminded her.

"And refused to mansplain it to me then," she snorted, hitching her purse strap on her shoulder. "As if I was too stupid to understand what men or people at this socioeconomic level think or feel. Honestly, I've had enough of this shit. I'm going to the penthouse."

She spun around and marched out of the room.

JW heard David groan and mutter under his breath. He couldn't make out the words but he did hear Diana's snort.

"You did too and you know it," she retorted. "Everyone treats her that way. I'm surprised she didn't just head to Maine after the attacks." He glanced around in time to see David's grimace. Diana stared at her husband. "She wanted to, didn't she? And you talked her out of it. Why?"

"Sweetheart," David started.

"Have fun," JW told him, before turning and going after Ally. *Dammit. She better not have gotten on the elevator yet.*

He didn't quite shift into a run, just a double-quick jog, and caught up with her as the doors opened. She didn't even look at him as she stepped inside. JW followed.

"Garage one," he told the operator.

"Yes, sir."

"Main lobby," Ally added.

"Belay that," JW stated, frowning at her. "We were going to talk, remember?"

"About what?" she wondered as if there was nothing he could say that she would want to hear.

For a moment, he stared at her as the elevator continued its descent.

"I would think you would prefer that be a private conversation," he murmured.

"Talking at all would be a novelty," replied Ally under her breath. Out of the corner of her eyes, she caught the smiles and knowing glances of the six others in the elevator. *They probably think it's a lovers' quarrel or something. If they only knew the truth. Of course, I don't know the truth. And I really doubt I'll get it.*

"I heard that," JW commented.

"Good."

Others got off at the main floor, but he held her back. With an exasperated sigh, she rolled her eyes.

"Seriously?" she muttered. "Fine. Five minutes, then I'm going home."

Once the elevator descended to the parking garage, he pulled keys from his back pocket as he guided her down the rows of vehicles. He bundled her into a gray SUV and sat behind the wheel. She simply sat there, hands folded on her lap, eyes steady on the cement block wall before her.

"I thought you had a full-time contract with the club," JW finally broke the silence.

Ally's cheeks flush with embarrassed heat.

"There were some issues. Liam agreed to my request to end it early." She shrugged. "I don't think I'm really a submissive anyway. No matter what the questionnaire results were."

"Why would you think you're not a submissive?" JW demanded. "You were perfect!"

"No," she contradicted him, shaking her head even as a rush of pleasure filled her at his compliment. "I tried. I really did, but it just didn't work out."

Scowling, he looked at her. His left arm was draped over the steering wheel and his fingers drummed the dashboard.

"Why on earth would you marry a man like Kevin MacLauren?" He demanded, frustration bubbling through his voice. "He's an absolute asshole."

She shook her head and looked out the side window, refusing to look at him.

"He was charming and a bit overwhelming. Before I knew it, we were in his plane flying to Vegas. As you might have deduced, David wasn't willing to break some male code of brotherhood to warn me about him, besides saying Kevin was always working a business angle." She snorted. "That applies to just about every man in this city, yourself included."

"Business has nothing to do with us," he told her in a low voice.

"No," she agreed softly. "Nothing had anything to do with us."

Stunned by her words and her determination to keep him at arm's length, JW could only stare at her. Then he felt sadness push in waves out of her. As she fumbled for the door handle, he reached out, caught her upper arms, and turned her to face him.

"Why would you think you're not a submissive?" he repeated.

"It just didn't work," Ally whispered. She swallowed, worked her jaw, and then sighed. "At least not the sex part. I tried all the usual therapies and thought one out of left field would work. I did gain the confidence and strength I didn't have before. I made friends with amazing people but, no," she shook her head, lifting her chin, "the boundaries of a submissive didn't work for me."

"Maybe that's why," he murmured.

Chapter Nine

"What is why?" Ally frowned.

The way he was looking at her made her uneasy, even as a rush of heat swept her body. She knew it would be totally unacceptable to throw herself at him and beg him to fuck her any way he wanted. *Besides, I'm stronger than that now. Aren't I?*

"Boundaries and safe words."

Frowning, she shook her head at his 'it's so obvious' tone.

"What do you mean? Submissives can…"

"Slaves can't," he reminded her.

Ally felt her jaw drop. *Slaves?*

"I was not and am not a slave," she stated, narrowing her eyes. *What game is he playing?*

JW's fingers traced her jaw. It took every bit of strength in her not to cuddle her cheek against his palm.

"Really? You practically were with me. I fucked you into exhaustion and didn't give you a chance to use your safe word," he continued, leaning toward her until their foreheads nearly touched. "Hell, I didn't even *ask* for your safe word. I used you like a slave, Ally. I took total control of your body, and you loved every minute of it. I did what I wanted. I could've done more and you wouldn't have tried to stop me."

His fingers lightly gripped her jaw and she swallowed nervously. Her pussy clenched at the reminder of their time together. He was right. About all of it. Did he understand that it was because of him? That she had given him everything of herself. She had completely trusted him and couldn't manage that with anyone else. Terrified that he might reject her, she remained quiet.

His eyes seemed to flicker and he smiled slightly. His left hand went to her knees, under her skirt and slid between her thighs. When his fingers brushed her damp panties, he chuckled softly in her ear. His right hand slid to the back of her head. Ally didn't move. JW had her completely in his control. The expression in his eyes told her that he knew it.

"I could do what I want with you right now, couldn't I? You would do anything I commanded if you thought I'd fuck you, wouldn't you?"

A shudder swept through her body and she closed her eyes at the flash of pleasure. He was right again. And from the timber of his voice, she could tell he relished the knowledge.

"Master," she whispered. "Please."

His finger pushed the cotton panties aside and stroked her folds. She gasped as his mouth covered hers. Two of his fingers slipped inside her pussy, hooking up and finding G-spot. His palm rubbed her clit. Feeling full, Ally moaned in his mouth as his tongue thrust into her in the same rhythm as his finger. Her hands came up and clutched at his sweater, tugging him closer. She felt the hunger rise and just when she was on the verge of orgasm, his fingers stilled and he raised his head.

Ready to beg, she opened her eyes and saw his triumphant expression. She knew what he would say before he spoke.

"No, slave. No orgasm until I give you permission." His voice was firm and stern.

My master.

"Yes, master," she replied, even as her pussy tightened around his fingers.

He gave her a knowing look as he removed his hand from between her thighs.

"Trying to get around me?" he whispered. "Hoping to convince me, slave?"

"No, master," she said quickly, shaking her head.

"Mmm hmm," answered JW, his right thumb stroking her neck. "Twelve hours. And you'll know what you really are."

"Yes, master," whispered Ally. If that's all she could have of him, she would take it.

JW couldn't have explained to anyone why he'd taunted Ally with being a slave. He couldn't understand the need to have her completely under his control again. And this time with absolutely no limits. He didn't want her to be able to refuse anything. Nothing violent or painful, but…he needed absolute control of something before his aggression overflowed in a destructive way. The need, the instinctive hunger to utterly dominate her. This scared the hell out of him. But it was the only thing he could do.

"Master?"

Her soft whisper brought him back to the present. Her fingers brushed the back of his hand. Calm certainty filled him. Without letting himself think about it another second, he started the engine and backed out of the parking space. Beside him, Ally kept silent, her hands clasped calmly on her lap. Her acquiescence stunned him. No protests, no argument, no demands.

Pulling out of the garage, he made a left and headed for the club. He fished his cell phone out of his coat pocket and punched several buttons.

"It's Master JW," he said before the person answering could say a word. "I'm coming in. I want a room for twelve hours."

"Of course, Master JW," the woman replied calmly. "Will you need anything?"

"Just the basics. Should be there in about ten minutes."

"Room seven-ten is available, sir. I'll send two slaves to ensure it's ready for your arrival. Parking space seventy-one."

"Perfect." He switched the phone off and dropped it in a cup holder. "We get there and there's no turning back or running away."

"I know."

Those dark eyes looked at him with trust and serenity.

Once in the underground garage of the club, JW parked in the assigned space, got out and moved swiftly around to open her door. Taking her by the waist, he lifted her out. She stood quietly as he closed the door and initiated the alarm. He turned to her and saw the shiver that swept her body. Instinct told him that she was even wetter than she had been when he'd fingerfucked her in the car. She would try to control her orgasms, but she was so on edge that eventually she would come without permission.

He took her by the elbow and headed swiftly for the elevator. He couldn't wait to push her as hard as he could. To make her willing to do anything to come. He wouldn't give her permission, of course. He'd already learned that she craved the punishment as much as the reward.

And he needed total control of her as much as she needed to give it to him.

That thought jolted him as they stepped into the elevator and he entered his code. The elevator rose, programmed to take them directly to the seventh floor. He didn't *want* a slave. Or a submissive. Certainly nothing permanent. Seeing Ally being mauled by Kevin MacLauren had been purely happenstance, and he wasn't above taking advantage of the situation, especially if it meant he got to fuck her again.

When the twelve hours was over, he'd go back to his cabin and she would stay at the club, accepting her true sexual nature.

JW ignored the sudden rage that reared its head at the idea of Ally being someone else's slave. That was simply the way things had to be. The way things *would* be. Because he sure as hell wasn't mentally fit to be anyone's master for more than short periods of time. He'd seen too much, done too much. He'd done what he had for his country, for his friend, but dealing with the nightmares was nearly more than he could handle. He sure as hell wouldn't subject someone else to them.

The elevator doors slid open and his fingers tightened on her arm as they walked down the hall.

"When we get in the room, take your clothes off quickly unless you want them torn off."

The tinge of threat got a reaction from her. Her head whipped around and he saw the dash of fear and excitement ripple in her eyes. He could just imagine how her pussy dripped.

At the door, he punched his code in and pushed through the entry quickly. Ally practically ran in and began stripping. He closed the door and leaned against it to watch her. He could see she had continued the mandated workouts for all club subs and slaves in her improved muscle tone. The softness of her curves was still there though, and his cock hardened as she carefully folded her clothes and put them on the dresser.

Straightening, she turned to face him.

"How would you like me, master?" she asked, a tremor in her voice.

Pushing away from the door, he removed his heavy coat and draped it across the chair to his right. Crooking his finger at her, he waited for her to cross the room to him. As soon as she was within arm's reach, he caught her upper arm and yanked her forward to slam into his chest.

He wanted to fuck her. No preliminaries, just straight fucking.

Turning, he pushed her back against the door and held her there with one hand lightly around her throat. His other hand worked his belt and zipper, then shoved his pants and briefs down to free his aching cock. Her breathing hitched under his palm and her soft

169

breasts bobbed. Giving in to his urges, he lowered his head to her tits and devoured the pale rose tips.

She cried out as her body arched off the door. He knew he was being rougher than he'd ever been with a woman, but he didn't care. He was going to let the animal out and she would just have to deal with it.

He worked his way from her breasts to her neck. Like a vampire, he sank his teeth into the delicate skin. She panted now, low mewling sounds coming from her mouth. Covering her breasts with his hands, he kneaded the already sensitive mounds and her body thrashed against his in response.

Knowing she had been on edge for a while, probably since she'd first seen him in the lobby, he gripped her thighs and pulled her legs wide.

"Look at me, Ally," his voice rasped in her ear.

With a gasp, she tried to lift her head, but just barely managed to meet his gaze.

"Don't come," he growled. "Not until I give you permission."

"Yes, master," she whispered weakly.

Her head lolled to the other side and he smiled. She wouldn't be able to hold back. Not the way he liked to fuck her. He remembered how she'd been that one night. She loved hard, wild fucking and that was exactly what she was going to get from him.

He bent his knees for the perfect angle to thrust his cock up and into her pussy.

Ally moaned against the fierce intrusion as he muscled his engorged flesh into her tight pussy. She had known she wouldn't be able to control herself. Not from the second she'd heard his voice. He came at her like a wild man and she reveled in it, even as she briefly wondered what it was about him that made her love the way he fucked her. As long as it was him.

Just like before. She closed her eyes as he fucked her, hips pounding rapidly against her flesh. He was hers for such a short time. *Just like before.* Well, she would make it memorable for both of them.

"Wrap your legs around my waist." His order was curt and he wouldn't be denied.

She managed to obey, hooking her ankles over his narrow hips. His cock slid deep and he stilled inside her pulsing flesh. She trembled, remembering what he'd done before. His hand pinched her nipple before gliding down her stomach.

"Master, please," she whimpered.

"Let's see how long you can hold out," he gritted, his breath fast and hot over her face.

"I won't. I can't. Please."

His thumb found her clit and she caught her breath. Opening her eyes, he was watching her face, gauging her reactions. He shifted his balance, forcing his cock deeper and hitting nerves she'd long thought dead. His thumb rubbed the swollen bud and the electricity built.

"Please. Please let me come. Please, master."

"Be a good slave," he crooned.

"I'm trying, but I…"

His mouth closed around her earlobe and nibbled. She moaned and her legs quivered around his waist from the effort of holding back her orgasm. His thumb made another circle then pressed hard against her arousal.

"Master, please…"

"No, slave. Don't come," he warned.

His tongue circled her ear and then his lips drifted along her neck. He pulled his cock slowly from her sheathe then drove back in as his fingers pinched her clit. The orgasm shot through her so fast her legs jerked away from his waist and her body arced off the door as the pulses of pleasure washed over her. She collapsed in his arms in the aftermath, unable and unwilling to care that she'd disobeyed him and earned a punishment. The sweet rush of euphoria overrode everything else.

Paradise. Heaven. Pure pleasure. That's all she felt. The world could collapse around them and she wouldn't care.

The low chuckle in her ear told her there was more to come. She'd earned a spanking. A harsh punishment because, given the still hard length in her pussy, he hadn't found his release.

"I'm sorry, master."

She hoped he wouldn't know it for the lie it was. She wasn't sorry. She'd wanted his cock in her pussy for months.

"Not yet," he replied, pulling out of her. "But you will be."

Taking a couple deep breaths to center herself, Ally lifted her head, saw his expression, and swallowed. His eyes gleamed and the left corner of his mouth tilted up. This would definitely be worse than before. And he was going to enjoy it. Nearly as much as she would.

He stepped back.

"Go to the side of the bed and lean your upper body on it. Spread your legs as wide as you can."

"Yes, master," she replied, standing as best as she could on legs that felt like limp noodles.

Tottering to the bed, she caught the bedpost to catch her balance. Putting her hands on the mattress, she stretched her torso on it. She was only five-four and, for her feet to touch the floor, her rib cage rested on the edge. She turned her head to face the headboard.

She could hear him remove his clothes and then his footsteps as he moved to the dresser. A drawer opened and closed, then another was opened. She bit her bottom lip as she realized he was looking for something in particular. As a submissive, she might have risked a peek and relied on her safe word if his choice was a hard limit for her.

Ally squeezed her eyes shut. As a slave, which he clearly considered her, she had no safe word, no limits, nothing. She could only trust him and hope he didn't do any real damage.

The weight of his body suddenly rose over her, pressing her against the mattress. Between her ass cheeks, his cock was still hard. She swallowed, her mind running wild, imagining what he could do to her. And she wanted him to do anything he wanted. She didn't care what it was or how depraved others might consider it. She wanted everything he could give her.

He lifted Ally and turned her over. Her master's hips pressed against her cunt as he hungrily feasted on her body. Nibbles, licks, fingers fondling everywhere—she writhed beneath him. Helpless, her pussy tightened again as his cock rubbed across her folds. She rolled her pelvis against his cock and he bit a nipple.

"Master," Ally's scream cut into the sexual tension. "Please!"

JW's head came up just enough so he could see her face. A hand came into her line of sight so she could see what he held: nipple clamps with chains connecting them. Ally couldn't move as her brain froze at the prospect of so much pleasure and pain. Her nipples seemed connected to her pussy, controlling her orgasms. He'd remembered that she had loved it when he tugged and pinched them.

Ally's breath caught in her chest. If he remembered that, had he thought of her? Had he wanted her since? If so, why didn't he come back to the club? Or contact Master Liam to have her sent to him?

Her eyes followed his hands as he tightened the hard rubber tips around her puckered nipples. Master tugged on the chain, then clipped a second chain to it, as the cool metal slid across her stomach.

Ally gasped as he pinched her clit, tugging it from under the protective hood. And then the clamp closed over the turgid flesh.

Pain shot through her body even as he stepped away and rolled her onto her tummy.

His hand splayed between her shoulder blades and she squeezed her eyes shut, knowing the blow was coming but unable to mentally prepare because she had no idea what he was using.

Thwack! She whimpered as the paddle landed on her right ass cheek. JW alternated between smacking her ass and upper thighs, his feet nudging her legs farther apart. To stay on the bed, she clutched at the bedspread. Even then, her body shifted and the nipple clamps bit in deep, tugging on the chain that ran to her clit.

Tears filled her eyes as he continued to spank her. She didn't sense any anger in him, just the steady controlled rise and fall of his hand. Ally couldn't feel his body heat any longer and bit her bottom lip. That was the worst part—the disconnect. The other time he'd spanked her, he'd been close so she could feel the brush of his leg, hip, or sometimes even his cock.

Her ass and thighs burned, and she realized that he was being careful. None of the smacks landed near her tailbone, where he might have caused nerve damage. There! His thigh touched hers as he gave her the last two spankings. She moaned and part of her relaxed. And grew hotter.

The paddle landed on the bed near her head. With blurry vision, she stared at it. His hands gripped her hips, lifting her right off the floor to meet his thrust. As his cock pushed into her pussy, she struggled to hold her upper body still.

"Do your tits burn as much as your ass?"

His voice sounded calm. Too calm. She wished she dared risk peeking at his face.

"Yes, master," she whimpered.

He pulled his swollen shaft nearly all the way out then drove into her pussy until she felt his balls against her heated skin. "Does your clit burn as much as your ass?"

"Yes, master," she sobbed as her body shifted and the chain pulled on the clamp. "Please, master. Please take them off."

His right arm snaked between her lower ribs and the bed, raising her chest slightly.

"No," he said in that still too calm voice.

Ally tried to brace her lower arms against the mattress as he fucked her. Each time he shafted into her weeping core, her clit caught between the weight of both their bodies and the bed. All while trapped by the clamp. The bundle of nerves screamed to be released. Her poor brain couldn't cope with the pain in her breasts and the fire in her ass. And shut down.

Somehow, she managed to hold herself still as he jackhammered his cock in and out of her. Ally shut everything out until he pushed her hair over her shoulder, making her neck available to his mouth. His chest brushed against her back a heartbeat before his lips and teeth began their own sweet torture against her flesh. Oh, God, she wanted more. She wriggled her hips against his, trying to pull him deeper, to keep him inside her. The heat consumed her and she wanted to throw herself into the flames.

"Master, please," she begged. "Please."

"You are not to come unless I give you permission," he grunted.

With a surge, he was still, pressing his solid hips into her ass. Ally felt his cock pump his release into her and squeezed her pussy muscles tight around him. The rigid flesh pulsed and throbbed until his orgasm receded.

"Good slave," he sighed. "You remembered to squeeze my dick with your cunt."

His lips were gentle now as he nuzzled her shoulder. His hands were light as he caressed her sides. Pulling his cock from her needy flesh, JW turned her over and released the clit clamp and then both nipple clamps at the same time. She gasped as the pain surged through the abused buds, then sighed as she felt the heat follow.

Weak from the fucking and the spanking, she slid off the edge of the mattress and collapsed at his feet. Leaving her there, he returned the paddle and clamps to the dresser. Coming back to the bed, his hand tangled in her hair and pulled her to her feet. Struggling to breathe, she stood quietly, her head hanging, until his hands caught her waist and lifted her onto the bed.

"On your back. Head on the pillows, stretch out your arms and legs."

As her mind cleared, Ally found herself strapped to the bed with a pillow near her hips. Blinking at this new action, she tracked his movements as he returned to the dresser. He came back with a blindfold. She watched his face until the cloth covered her eyes, hoping to read his expression and fighting despair when she saw nothing at all.

"Master?"

Now unable to see, she had no choice but to trust him. And prayed that when it was all over, he wouldn't leave her the way he had before. Deep in her heart, she knew he would. JW wouldn't let her in. He didn't want anyone in. She'd seen the quick reaction to his grandfather's words about her. The sudden tension in his body, nostrils flaring and eyes narrowing. No, he didn't want anything more from her than answering their physical needs in this room. Beneath the blindfold, Ally closed her eyes as the tears slipped out in time with the beats of her broken heart.

She heard the hum of the vibrator and the tip brushed the inside of her thigh. He was going to push her. Push her into having more orgasms without permission. What she didn't understand was why.

As the vibrator caressed her damp and swollen folds, she knew the cycle was just beginning and could have wept from frustration.

JW watched Ally as he moved the dildo in and out of her pussy. She obviously struggled to keep her orgasms at bay. It was inevitable. He would drive her over the edge repeatedly as she begged for permission. He'd spank her, then fuck her mouth or her ass, or both. He glanced at the clock over the door. He could do this for a few hours, let her sleep, then start up again. He would give her permission to come only near the end as he fucked her pussy for the last time.

JW woke at peace for the first time in years. The warm and exhausted woman in his arms was the reason. Tightening his hold on her, he thought hard about his next decision. His cock had other ideas, already stiffening against Ally's rounded bottom. He'd never be able to think if he stayed in the room with her.

Carefully, he eased from the bed and brought the covers over her shoulders. She stirred slightly, then wriggled back slightly to the warmth where he'd been. Smoothing her hair off her face, he studied her for a moment.

Such a small woman, yet so strong. He'd been three years ahead of Kevin MacLauren in the elite prep school they'd attended but remembered him as a bully. His eyes narrowed as he recalled the incident that had gotten Kevin and others expelled. They'd beaten a scholarship student nearly to death and left him in the woods around the school. He wasn't surprised that Kevin hadn't recognize him. The stigma of his illegitimacy had hung over him and he'd been a loner even then. Of course, his appearance had changed from a tall, lanky teenager with hair halfway down his back to a tall, muscular man with short hair and combat weariness in his eyes.

And Ally had been married to Kevin. Having heard bits of gossip over the years, JW could only imagine what that had been like. Kevin wasn't known for being a considerate lover or gentleman. His family name and money had shielded him from the ramifications of his actions. So far.

Ally sighed in her sleep and JW was tempted to crawl back into bed with her. Clenching his jaw, he forced himself to step back. Quickly pulling on his sweater, jeans, and boots, JW slipped out of the room.

A drink. He needed a drink. He needed to think this through. He stalked down the hall to the stairs. A few moments in the pub and he'd figure things out.

****

Something was different, but Ally's tired brain couldn't figure it out. Shivering slightly, she tugged the comforter over her shoulder and then stopped. Where was Master JW?

Heart in her throat, she took a breath. "Master? Master, are you here?"

When there was only silence, she forced herself to sit up and look around the room. The bathroom door was open, the room beyond dark. She was alone.

She slumped forward, fingers tightening on the covers. Again. *Damn him!* He'd left her alone again. Tears filled her eyes and slid down her cheeks. She'd felt their connection, hoping he had as well, especially when he'd pulled her close and fallen asleep. And…nothing. She really had been nothing more than a fuckfest for him. Twice.

"Dammit, Ally," she muttered, swinging her legs over the edge of the mattress. "Fool me once, shame on you. Fool me twice, shame on me." As soon as her feet reached the floor, she collapsed to the floor.

"No. No. I'm not falling apart. Not here. Not now. Not again."

Pulling herself back onto the bed, she reached behind the nightstand and found the intercom button.

"Hello? This is Master Seamus."

"Hello, Master Seamus," she replied. "I'm submissive Ally. I, uh, the master has left and…well, I need help leaving."

"Ally, I don't have you on the listing. Who was with you?"

"Master JW, sir."

"I see the room number now. I'll have a guard and a slave there in a few minutes, Ally."

"Thank you, sir," she whispered.

She crawled to the dresser, used the drawers to pull herself up to reach her clothes. Her mind numb, she automatically started getting dressed. In moments, a guard and slave opened the door. The guard stayed at the door while the slave silently helped her with her clothes. The brown-clad woman kept her eyes down but reached out and squeezed Ally's hand. Grateful for the gesture, Ally returned the pressure briefly as she stood by the dresser.

"I'm ready," she whispered, then cleared her throat when she realized the guard couldn't hear her. "I'm ready," she repeated, louder.

He turned his head, understanding in his expression.

"Master Seamus called a taxi for you. It should be outside."

"Thank you," she replied, nodding as the slave helped her move forward.

Much as she had in April, she stumbled on the sidewalk and collapsed into the seat as Seamus O'Grady gave the driver her address.

"Ally?" he inquired, voice full of concern.

"Thank you for the assistance," she whispered, closing her eyes as the taxi pulled away. *I will not break down. I will not fall apart. There are too many people around who would ask too many questions and it would be more humiliating than what Kevin did to me.*

Finally reaching the penthouse, she left a note for Carla saying she wasn't feeling well and needed to sleep. Locking her bedroom door, she removed her clothes as she walked across to the bed. Curled up under the duvet, she shuddered, then the sobs came. To muffle the sound of her wailing, she pressed her face against the pillow.

****

JW stood outside the door, still unable to believe he was going to do it. He tapped in the code, opened the door, and froze. The bed was empty, the sheets and blankets hanging off the side. A glance at the dresser she'd put her folded clothes on told him that her things were gone as well. His hand gripped the door frame. She was gone. This time *she* had left without a word.

Fighting back the emotions he'd only just admitted to himself, he went to the chair, picked up his coat, and left.

Chapter Ten

"Ally?"

Lifting her head from the pillow, Ally saw her cousin and Diana framed by the door. Still trapped in the submissive mindset, she rolled out of bed, keeping her eyes down. Swearing, David was there in a heartbeat. Kneeling next to her, he pulled her against him.

"Fuck," he whispered, one hand holding her head to his shoulder. "Don't do this, Ally. Don't do this to us."

She just shook her head. With a groan, he lifted her off the floor and tucked her back under the blanket. Diana came to stand by the bedside while he got the chair for her.

"You've lost so much weight," the English rose breathed. "Are you refusing to eat or is this some sort of internal club thing?"

"Not hungry," murmured Ally weakly, curling under the covers.

Sitting on the edge of the bed, David stared at her. His eyes pleaded with her, his fists clenched on his thighs.

"Ally, why are you doing this?" Distress rang clear in his voice. Self-blame in his expression. "Is it because of MacLauren? I'm sorry for how I reacted—"

"It's not because of him," she denied, then sighed. "He's a part of all of it, but not this."

"Were you mistreated?" probed Diana.

"Not a bit," Ally insisted. "Everyone has been extraordinarily kind to me."

"Not everyone if you're behavior is this drastic," David growled.

"There was a master," she relented, determined to not say the name. "I got attached to him, but he doesn't feel the same way. I can't stay here and chance seeing him." *I can't resist him, but he doesn't care about me in anyway. I have to leave. I have to make sure I won't see him again.*

"Then come home with us," Diana proposed, her hand catching at Ally's fingers. "You don't have to go anywhere you don't want to or see anyone you don't want to. You could go back to Maine to regroup. But don't do this. Please."

Tears filled Ally's eyes as she gazed at Diana. *The last time I'll see her. Unless my new master is very generous.*

"Ally," David said urgently. "Who is he?"

"No, David," she replied, closing her eyes. "I won't tell you."

"Fuck," he muttered.

Diana's fingers tightened.

"Please, Ally," she begged, emotion choking her voice. "Don't do this. Come home with us."

Giving her hand a final squeeze, Ally pulled her fingers out of reach under the blankets. David finally sighed and stood.

"Diana, let's go."

"David, we can't…"

Ally heard the chair scrape on the floor as if David was pulling his wife bodily from it.

"We can't change her mind," David said. "Ally, if you ever need us, call. No matter when or where, we'll be there for you."

She didn't know if he saw her slight nod. The door closed a second later.

****

JW rolled over and pulled the pillow over his head at the noise. The pounding continued for several minutes. Finally, it stopped, only to be replaced by his cell phone ringing.

"Goddammit!" he yelled, flinging the pillow across the room toward the dresser where his phone sat.

The pillow barely made it to the end of the bed. It balanced on the railing before rolling out of sight. As it plopped on the floor, the ringing continued. Muttering every foul oath he'd learned since Basic Training, JW jerked from the bed and stalked over to the offending device. At the thumping his prosthesis made on the floor, he absently realized he'd forgotten to take it off.

"What the hell do you want?" he barked into the receiver, glancing at the clock and seeing it was nearly noon.

"Open your damned door or I'll break it down and then break your fucking neck," Liam O'Grady growled back at him.

"What the fuck is your problem?" JW demanded.

"Open the damned door."

The phone went silent but the pounding began again.

Continuing his oaths of rage, JW marched out of the bedroom through the living area and unlocked his door. Liam was through the portal and swinging before he'd taken two steps back.

Only instincts honed through years of training and battle kept JW's head out of the way so the fist glanced across his temple and not his nose.

"What the fuck is your problem?" he yelled, quickly backing away from the enraged man.

Kicking the door shut, Liam stalked after him. JW thought he saw snow flurries beyond him before the thud closed out the cold.

"I don't want to see your ass in the club ever again," snarled his distant cousin.

"I'll say it a third time since you didn't seem to hear me. What the fuck is your problem?" JW growled right back.

Liam got close, right up in his face.

"Ally. She barely had a clue what was going on the first time. But this second time..." As if realizing how close he was to swinging again, Liam turned away, running a hand through his reddish-brown hair. "I was in Ireland and got delayed by business and weather or I would have been on your ass days ago. What the hell were you thinking? She responds to nothing and no one!"

"I spanked her and...I was careful with her," JW defended himself. "And she enjoyed the fucking. Trust me."

"That's what she said," Liam confirmed with a sigh, looking out the front window. "And each fucking time, you left her alone after," Liam fumed, pacing back and forth. "You can't fucking do that. It screws with a submissive's mind like nothing else."

"I didn't leave her." JW stated, stepping forward, hands clenching into fists. "I went down to the pub to clear my mind so I could think, but when I came back up, *she* was gone."

"Ah, shit. Are you serious?"

Now near the door, Liam turned.

"Completely. Ask Tom, he was tending the bar. I left my coat in the room. I didn't leave her." JW got defensive. He hadn't done anything wrong.

Liam studied him a moment and JW felt distinctly uneasy. The other man had a way of coming out with some crazy shit about a person when he looked at them like that.

"How much have you been drinking?" Liam finally asked.

"What the hell does that have to do with anything?" JW demanded in bewilderment.

"I can smell it," Liam replied, going through the cabin to the kitchen. He lifted the lid to the trash can and shook his head. "I'm seeing lots of bottles and nothing that looks like it contained food." He looked over his shoulder at JW. "Well, that explains why you look like shit."

JW frowned and glanced down at himself, only now realizing he was naked. He could tell he'd lost weight as his ribs and hip bones protruded more than they had...however many days ago.

"Yeah, um..."

"Congratulations, JW. You broke her. She doesn't care what happens to her. Nothing anyone says to her can change her mind. Not even David and Diana were able to reach her." Liam walked into the living area, standing behind the couch. "She wants to be put up for a contract. As a slave. She doesn't care to whom, what their reputation is, or what they end up doing to her."

JW blinked. *What the hell?* His head spun and he grabbed at the back of the chair to stay balanced.

"No," he denied the statement. *A slave. That's what I called her. How I treated her.*

"David came to see me after they talked to Ally this morning. He is spitting fire and ready to strangle you. He said Ally wouldn't reveal your name, but he put it together from the way you two acted at the meeting ten days ago." Liam smiled slightly. "After you brought her to the club, Ally left for two days, came back requesting her old room, and hasn't left it the past week. Dare," he referred to his cousin who was a doctor, "is seriously worried about her health and actually forced an IV on her to keep her hydrated. I'd stay out of his reach as well as David's." He sighed. "Normally, her contract would be one of the highest priced. Everyone knows her, likes her. She has an excellent reputation at the Shadows, even with those who know her history with Kevin. But now?" He shook his head. "I put her on display and everyone will laugh at the idea of bidding on her. She's a mess. She's simply given up and there's nothing anyone can do to reach her. Not even when Alice told her Madison was going to buy her contract—"

"No!" JW launched himself at Liam and drove him against the wall. His forearm pressed against his friend's throat. "You're not doing this."

"She's broken, JW. Was that your goal? Because you've exceeded beyond anything I've ever seen or heard, you fucking sadist. Not even what 'Kevin the Asshole' did destroyed her like this."

"You can stop this. You *will* stop this," JW insisted.

"It's none of your business anymore," Liam told him, tone and face almost bored.

"I'm fucking making it my business," he growled, thinking Liam was pretty damn calm considering JW could kill him in five seconds.

"Why?" Liam asked pointedly.

"When is the display?" JW demanded, his mind spinning out wild ideas that were crazier each second.

"Read your damn emails," Liam told him. "You got to her, JW. And I think she got to you. Something connected between the two of you. I could see it in her that first time. She's been worried about you since she met you. Don't scoff or sneer," Liam warned before JW could do more than open his mouth. "She's gone through her own hell. She lost her father when she was nine. Then she lost her mother, uncle, and grandfather in a car accident hours after she graduated from college. Then 9/11 happened in plain sight of the Brown penthouse. She heard the first plane hit and saw the second one. Top it off, she was married to Kevin. And we all know what an asshole he is. It might not be the same as your hell, but we all have our own demons."

Shoving away from him, JW stomped around the living room. Liam massaged at his throat, which brought him some satisfaction.

"I don't suppose you'd consider putting on clothes?" Liam asked. "Or put the thermostat above freezing?"

"No one invited you here," JW growled, still struggling to cope with what Liam had told him.

For something to do, he strode into the kitchen and started making coffee. Some part of him winced when he saw the trash can overflowing with bottles. *What the hell does he think I can do for her? I'm broken. Hollow. I'm not even whole anymore.* To emphasize that point, he stamped his artificial foot on the floor. *What kind of woman would choose me? I've seen too much. Done too much.*

"You don't have to fight your demons on your own," Liam said quietly, almost gently. "You don't have to be alone in your hell on this earth. Something about you helped her for a time. And I think something about her helped you."

"Fuck," muttered JW, turning away and closing his eyes. "Yeah, whatever. I'm dealing with it."

"Really?" Liam walked to stand on the other side of the breakfast bar that separated the kitchen from the living area. "How's that going for you?"

"No one can help me with this. With any of this," JW stated, hearing the bitterness in his voice. All he could hear was Kevin's voice jeering that he wasn't a whole man. All he could see were the startled looks before people turned away in embarrassment.

"Bullshit." Again, Liam spoke in a mild voice, a tinge of Irish accent that he always had after one of his trips.

"Liam, you don't *know*," JW spun to face him. "None of you have a fucking clue what it's like."

"Her grandfather survived the Battle of the Bulge. His best friend died in his arms after they killed a dozen Germans," Liam stated in a matter-of-fact tone.

That drew JW up short.

"How would you know that?"

"She told me after your first time together at the Shadows," Liam nodded. "Yeah, I've actually had conversations with her, JW. Have you? Do you know anything about her? How old she is? What she studied in college? What she wants to do or be? Or do you just want her as a fuck-toy? Ready to spread her legs or drop to her knees at the snap of your fingers." Liam snorted, his expression one of disgust. "From what I've picked up from her and what Seamus, the guard and slave who went to help her told me, you treated her as a slave. You used her to fuck yourself dry and left her like a discarded whore."

"Don't talk about her like that," JW growled, hating the way Liam's words rang true. He didn't know much about Ally's life, but he knew *her*. He knew she was smart, quick-witted, with a sense of humor. She was strong, tough, yet gentle and calm. "She's not a whore and I did not leave her."

"JW, were you in the room when she woke up? Did you tell her you'd be back shortly and to stay in the room?"

Staring at the coffeemaker as it gurgled to life, JW clenched his jaw, knowing he'd fucked up. He'd assumed she would just be there, and assumptions got people killed. Or worse. *What have I done to Ally?*

Liam sighed.

"Maybe I shouldn't have come here," he murmured, as if more to himself than JW. "I just, shit, I just thought that you'd recognize and admit to the connection between the two of you. That you'd accept responsibility for what you have done to her."

"Liam, I'm broken. I'm not even a whole man," JW reminded him, lifting his right leg and tapping the metal. "If anything, I'm the stereotypical veteran from the movies, wallowing in post-traumatic stress and drinking to forget. No woman would want to be around me."

"She wouldn't care about the leg. Did she even look at it? Or seem to notice?" Liam pressed, as if he knew the answer.

Frowning, JW considered that, then grimaced and shook his head.

"I'm not sure I gave her the chance to see it."

"Her uncle did three tours in Nam. He was injured by a landmine and lost his lower left leg and some fingers."

Reaching for a mug, JW froze as the words hit him. Blindly, he grabbed the first from the shelf as he reviewed everything Liam had told him. *Jesus, she had to have known about the leg when she saw me before the meeting. She was pissed at me for leaving her. About not calling her or something. She knew what had happened, what I was missing, and it didn't matter to her. She didn't act that way during the meeting because of MacLauren but because she felt something for me. Holy shit.* The idea staggered him.

"She hasn't gone through it, JW, but she's loved those who have. The woman has more empathy and heart than ninety percent of the people you'll ever run into."

JW stared at Liam, surprised by the admiration in his voice.

"And I fucked her up," JW whispered in shock and self-recrimination, realizing just what he'd done to her. He poured the coffee and gestured as he left the kitchen. "Help yourself."

"I'll be up for a month the way you make it," Liam complained, moving past him to get his own mug. "It's not too late."

"Meaning?"

"Bid on her tomorrow night. Take her contract."

"Jesus, Liam," JW breathed. He paced around, deliberately letting his prosthesis clump on the wooden floor. "Look at me, I'm barely fit to be around people. How can I can be trusted as a master? You just said you were going to expel me." He paused at the back door, glanced over his shoulder, and shook his head. "Those two times with her…God help me, all I wanted to do was fuck us both into exhaustion."

"You certainly did that," Liam confirmed, sipping and wincing at the coffee's strength. "JW, think about the effect you had on her. She was married to Kevin MacLauren for cryin' out loud! I can't imagine he gave a shit about her satisfaction or her emotions in general."

"The man is a dick," grumbled JW.

"Well, yeah, most people would agree to that," Liam drawled, walking to the leather couch and sitting down. "JW, be honest with me. You felt better with her than you have since the last time you saw her. Didn't you? You don't know why. She doesn't know why. And that's okay." JW turned around and Liam held up a hand for silence. "After your first time with Ally, I could see a difference in her that wasn't there before. I've seen it in subs who gain confidence after a good session with a master. Ally sure as hell didn't have it when she came to the club. God, if you'd seen her then. Tim Jones was right. It worked for her. *With you.* Then three days later, after you and Parker had to leave early, Madison dragged her out of the selection room, and the submissives nearly shouted the place down to keep her safe."

"Madison did what?" JW snarled.

"And I assigned her to demonstrations and classes, with the caveat that no one fucked her," Liam continued in a matter-of-fact tone.

JW held himself still. Had he heard Liam correctly?

"Why?"

"I was hoping you'd come back to the club," answered his friend. "Yeah, it's probably not an officially approved therapy, but I thought it was worth a shot."

JW saw the expression on the other man's face and scowled.

"I don't want your pity."

"It's not pity. It's concern." Liam leaned forward, resting his forearms on his thighs. "JW, you need something to…" he paused as if searching for the right word, "to take care of. To attach to. Whether she was there at the right time and place or whatever the reason, you were there for her as well. You gave her protection and security in a world that's lost its mind. If it had any sanity to begin with," he admitted wryly.

"Two lost souls wandering the night who just happen to cross paths?" JW frowned. Was it possible? He remembered how he'd felt that first time he'd seen her, when she'd put a hand on his arm, whispering for him to be safe. That had been when he'd had the vision of the explosion. *Shit. I misunderstood all of that. Ally is who I thought of when it happened. Not Mom or anyone else. Ally.* "We had a connection immediately," he murmured. "I rejected it. I left her that night in the garden." He took another drink, smiling as Liam did the same and grimaced. "After 9/11, at the party Grandmother had. That's when we first met. I kissed her. I couldn't help it. What I felt," JW shook his head. "It was more than I'd ever felt before."

"Yeah, I know," Liam told him with a dry glance. "It was like an earthquake."

"You felt it?" That startled JW.

"I did," came the confirmation. "I'd say it's safe to say your mother and Gisele did as well at the least. The younger ones might not have understood it."

"They've never said a word."

"They wouldn't," Liam pointed out. "Not unless you brought it up. And you shut it down very quickly."

"I had to."

The younger ones might not have, but Mom sure as hell would. Why didn't she say anything? Why didn't she contact Ally and have her come when I was wounded?

"Why?" demanded Liam.

"I was about to walk into combat, Liam. The last thing I needed—"

"Was an emotional tether?" came the quiet, almost mocking, question.

"How would starting a relationship or even thinking it have been a good idea?" JW challenged. "For either of us? I didn't know if I'd be alive in seventy-two hours. I had to focus everything on the missions I'd be given. Or I'd be dead and Parker along with me."

"You still thought about her though, right?"

JW glared at him. Liam shook his head.

"You remember Christmas two years ago?" Liam asked.

Puzzled at the change in subject, JW just nodded.

"Your family's Christmas party," came the prompt. "David proposed to Diana?"

"Yeah, pissed off her family," JW replied with a smile at the memory.

"They had just met the night before," Liam told him. "David proposed to her inside twenty-four hours of meeting her. They met that Friday night, saw each other Saturday afternoon, and he proposed as soon as he saw her Saturday night. The third time they were together."

JW frowned. "Are you saying I should have proposed to Ally the night I met her? Liam, for fuck's sake, I was leaving the next morning—"

"Oh, for Christ's sake," muttered Liam, adding a few curses in Gaelic for good measure. "JW, you have the gift. You've heard the connection talked about by family members who have felt it. You've felt it. And you didn't do a damn thing when the connection was made. David heard a few things from me and Aunt Zoey and took a leap of faith. He didn't deny it. He didn't delay it. He didn't make a bunch of shitty excuses for not acting on it. And he's happy. He's got the love of his life. You rejected it. You pushed it away. You *left* it. Not once or twice but three fucking times!"

"I told you I—"

"Shut the fuck up," yelled Liam. "Stop making excuses. Stop it already, will you? You're driving me up a fucking wall."

Stunned, JW snapped his jaw shut and stared at him. For a long moment, Liam glared at him, heaving in three deep breaths.

"The day after you arrived stateside after rescuing Ben," he finally spoke, quieter. "She asked to see me. I thought she was going to ask to go back to the selection room and I was trying to figure out a way to keep her out of there. She asked about you. She wanted to know if I knew how you were."

JW's body froze. *I thought she learned about it in the papers.*

"You told her what happened?"

"I told her what little I knew. She asked, if I had the chance and thought it appropriate, to let you know she was worried about you."

"Why the fuck didn't you tell me then?" JW roared. He wasn't sure which was spinning out of control more—his heart or his mind—at everything he was hearing.

"Because I hoped you'd ask for her yourself. That having been so close to death you'd want to live. To love. To be with the one person, besides your mother, who brings you peace. Who centers you in a way not even Zoey can." Liam gazed at him and now JW saw the bewilderment. "Good God, man, how were you able to walk away from her three times? Destiny's given you more chances than it usually gives anyone, and you are *still* refusing to accept the gift. It's as if you're being deliberately cruel to her to protect yourself. And all you've done is deny both of you something precious that you both need."

"I was about to go into hell or back into it," JW defended himself. "The last thing I needed was a woman—"

"Waiting for you? Besides your mother, of course. Has it occurred to you that she was waiting anyway? That she was the reason you stayed focused out there so you could come home to her?"

JW snorted.

"Yeah, sure she was waiting. Weeks later, she flew off to Vegas with Kevin the Asshole."

"If you'd spoken to her, written to her, I'll bet you anything she wouldn't have."

Clenching his jaw, JW took a deep breath. He hated it when Liam spoke sense like that. The man knew people better than anyone. Yeah, he'd taken psychology and all those mental mumbo-jumbo classes, but he had instincts. He always had. Fear rose up like bile in his throat. *Slowly. Take this slowly. Dip a toe into the waters.*

"Just who knows about the auction?"

Liam grimaced and JW's gut clenched. He'd been hoping he was the first Liam had notified.

"Since I was in Ireland, Ally talked to Seamus. He gave her the forty-eight-hour waiting period and then he emailed all unattached Doms." At his glance, JW braced himself for the other shoe to drop. "And the board, of course."

"What? The board? Shit!"

Mom. His mother's face when he'd walked into the meeting with Ally came to mind. She had approved of Ally, especially the way Ally had defended him. *Oh, Mom is going to fucking kill me.*

Sipping his coffee, Liam smirked.

"Yeah, it's procedure. Zoey called me about it before I'd even read the email. I barely talked her out of coming up here and talking to you. She likes Ally. A lot. And not just because she was ready to take on her ex when he insulted you, but for how she's come through what life has thrown at her and hasn't let it warp her." Liam's gaze swept JW's nude form then glanced at the trash can. "I can imagine Zoey's reaction to your activities the past week."

"Then don't tell her," JW winced, not needing to imagine his mother's words.

She wouldn't need to say a thing. One look from her and I'm five years old again, caught trying to put tadpoles and frogs in everyone's bathtubs. The memory of that spanking, one of the few he'd received from her, made his butt clench.

"I'll think about it," Liam drawled, green eyes twinkling before he got serious again. "Madison has already stated that he intends to bid."

JW growled at the thought. *No fucking way is that asshole getting his hands on my Ally.* "Why don't you just dismiss his ass and be done with him?"

"Believe me, I wish I could," replied Liam wearily. "But rules are rules, and he is still a member of the board." Liam snorted. "David's having an easier time cleaning house than I am."

"You can't choose your family," muttered JW.

"Yeah, but you can choose your friends," Liam agreed with a nod. "I think I can convince most of the others that this is a tantrum of sorts, a conflict between you and Ally, and you're handling it. So, it will probably just be you and Madison bidding."

"And I've deeper pockets than Madison," JW smiled tightly. He'd empty his entire trust fund if he had to.

"Oh, he can't go that high despite his bragging and intimidation of some of the other interested parties. Since he tried to drag Ally out of the submissive's selection room, his businesses have been taking some pretty big hits. Rumors have been spreading.

Ugly rumors." The two men shared a satisfying smile. JW understood exactly what Liam meant—those within the Shadows were excluding Madison, and even without knowing the reasons, others in the business world and their society had taken note and followed their lead. "So, can I put you down as an attendee for the auction? Or should I tell Ally I've changed my mind about having it?"

"What do you think her reaction would be to that?" JW wondered, realizing Liam had spent more time with Ally than he had. In many ways, he knew how she thought better than JW did.

Frowning, Liam considered that a moment and shook his head.

"I'm not sure," he finally answered. "She's in a fragile state. Probably worse than when David brought her to the club in April. My first inclination is that she would bolt home to Maine and not come back to the city unless David desperately needed her for the company."

"You don't think she would stay? Like she did after Kevin?"

It felt weird, asking Liam about her reaction, but JW knew the other man was most likely to know.

"Nope," came the prompt answer. "Kevin took a massive hit at her pride, but you, JW, you managed to break her heart when she didn't even realize her heart was involved." Liam snorted. "Then again, you denied yours was involved, so who should be surprised?"

"That horse is dead so drop the stick already," JW growled.

"Not until you tell me what you're going to do about this."

"You sure you can keep everyone else from bidding on her?" JW asked, worried about that. *There are a few who could beat me.*

"Yeah, I can do that. Those more into exhibition will probably still show up to see her, but I can't stop that. Quite a few will show up just to see Madison get beaten."

JW wrestled with his fury at other men and women seeing Ally naked. *It will be the absolute last time. A last lesson for both of us.* Getting up, he went to the kitchen and poured more coffee as his mind spun out the plan.

"I need Bron in on this as well. After she's on display, you take her into your office to sign the paperwork. If she reads the contract before signing," he shrugged. "But if she doesn't," he smiled and looked at Liam. "Then she'll earn a spanking."

"Of course," he replied, nodding, then frowning. "Wait a minute. Why are you bringing Bronson into the middle of this?"

"As well as going over the contract, which I'll have some adjustments made to, I'll need a prenup for her to sign. Bron can handle that." *And I'll give him a couple bottles for the liquor cabinet.*

"Holy shit," breathed Liam. "Are you serious? Marriage?"

JW sipped his coffee and smiled.

"Alrighty then, I'll take care of that. You call Bron. But first, could you go take a shower and get dressed?" Liam asked.

"I've always wondered what you were into," JW threw at him as he headed for the bathroom.

"Not you, that's for damn sure. I'm going home. Get your ass in gear." Liam laughed as he turned for the front door.

****

Ally stared up at the ceiling.

Tears flooded her eyes. It was six o'clock. In two hours, she would be put on display for a permanent slave contract. She held out no hope that JW would decide he wanted her. Why should she even consider it? He'd left her twice, three times if she included the first time they met, and the only reason there had been a second time in the club was because of sheer coincidence.

She curled up on the bed and let all the pent-up emotions out. Better to cry her fill now so she had a chance to recover. She knew how puffy and red her eyes got when she cried. When there were no more tears, she got up, showered, and cupped cold water in her hands to her eyes to reduce the swelling. Moments before eight, she gave her long dark hair a final brushing and pulled on a silver cloak. She stepped into the hall and found Master Liam waiting.

"Are you ready?" he said, his voice stiff and formal.

"Yes, Master Liam." She kept her words low and equally proper.

He hesitated a moment then nodded.

"Follow me."

Staying silent, Ally walked at his side down the hall to the elevator. The doors opened as they approached. Entering, he punched in the code and stood in silence as they went down to the second floor. He took her elbow and guided her down the corridor, paused to enter another code, and then put her on a four-foot diameter dais. Turning her around, he tilted her chin.

"Last chance," he warned.

In silent response, Ally raised her hands and released the clasp of her cloak meeting his gaze defiantly. The silver silk puddled around her feet. She saw his lips press together before he nodded and left the room. Slowly, the dais began to turn.

Startled, she realized that she was already on display. The room was circular with mirrored panels about six feet wide. She could see only her own reflection, but the potential bidders saw every inch of her.

Taking a deep breath, she gathered up all her courage and forced her knees to straighten and her chin to stay level. Unable to deal with the multiple images of herself, she closed her eyes, focusing on breathing. She lost track of time, but finally Master Liam returned as the dais stopped spinning. Worried, she accepted his hand to step down.

"Did..." she faltered as he bent to pick up her cloak. "Did someone choose me?"

He swept the material over her shoulders and secured the toggle. Without a word, he left the small room. Startled, she hurried after him to his office across the hall. He sat down at his desk and gestured for her to sit in the chair opposite.

"This is your slave contract," he told her, pushing a folder across to her. "Once you sign at the tabs, that's it."

Nodding, she picked up the pen to her right and opened the folder. Nearly blind from sudden tears, she looked for the tabs and signed her name four times. Putting the pen down, she closed the folder and put her hands in her lap, keeping her gaze on her fingers. *It's done.*

"Damn," he muttered, slapping the desk. "All right then. Fuck."

As the door behind him opened, he stood and Ally scrambled to her feet. Weaving from stress-induced exhaustion and self-imposed starvation, she weaved and black spots danced before her eyes.

"Ally!"

As if from a distance, she heard the one voice she'd longed for just before she collapsed to the floor. Ally tried in vain to open her eyes but it took too much energy. Warmth cocooned her, and she was lifted by strong arms. Under her head, she heard a steady heartbeat.

"I'll punish you in the morning, slave," a man whispered.

"Yes, master," she sighed, before darkness overwhelmed her.

Holding her weakened body, JW cursed himself for what she'd been through the past fifteen months. All because he hadn't had the guts to stay with her that evening. To talk to her, to ask her to write to him, to wait and see what developed when he could see her.

Bron and Grant stood uneasily on either side of him. Liam, Seamus, and Ben witnessed the prenuptial agreement. With Ally in his arms, JW stood, cradling her to his chest.

"Thank you," he said quietly to the men.

Bron gathered up the paperwork, placed it in a briefcase and closed it, snapping the locks into place. Taking the handle, Bron looked at JW as Grant took Ally's cloak and draped it over her body.

"Ready?" the lawyer asked.

Nodding, JW started for the door. Seamus jumped ahead of him, opening it, then going ahead to push the elevator button. Only his cousins walked farther with him. Stepping out of the elevator first, Grant had the key to the silver SUV and unlocked the passenger door, stepping back. Carefully, JW placed Ally on the seat, pulling the strap over her and clicking it into place. Reaching into the back, he grabbed a blanket and tucked it around her before lowering the seat so she reclined. Straightening, he faced his cousins.

"Thank you," he repeated.

"Glad we could help," Bron told him, handing him the briefcase, which JW put under Ally's feet.

"And we've learned lessons," Grant added, giving him a quick embrace and thump on the back, "from your mistakes. It's been a while since you did that for any of us."

"Glad to be of service," JW drawled, hugging Bron with a thump

As they stepped back from the new SUV his grandparents had given him, JW walked around, got in, and started the engine. Returning their waves with one of his own, he pulled forward to leave the underground parking garage. With the first snowstorm of the season starting to make itself felt, the streets were mostly deserted. JW was glad of that as he made good time leaving the city.

He wanted to get Ally home before the full force of mother nature struck.

Home. He had a home. And he wanted Ally to see it. To like it. To fall in love with it the way he had. The need for her to like it, to love it, made him nervous. As he left the city lights behind, he smiled, remembering the conversation with his mother a few hours earlier.

After making a prearranged stop, he arrived at the Franklin mansion late that afternoon. His mother was waiting in the foyer and pounced as soon as he walked through the door. He had barely been able to wave at his grandmother before Zoey had dragged him into the library and closed the door.

"You felt a connection with her. Felt it before you even saw her face," she said in a voice full of disappointment. *"You felt the fire when she touched your arm. Before you kissed her. And you just left her? Without a word? JW, how could you? That's not how you treat a woman, especially one…"* In disgust, she'd stalked away from him to stare out at the snowflakes coming down. *"I couldn't believe it when I saw that email from Seamus. After that meeting, it was the last thing I expected. When you ran after her, after defending her the way you did—"*

"And you," he interjected. *"I was defending you as well, Mom."*

Zoey flashed him a knowing glance over her shoulder.

"Bullshit, son. Yes, some of it might have been for me, but your anger toward Kevin was ready to explode. Gisele and I felt it

when you first saw him in the lobby." She turned completely to face him. "I'm not sure which surprised me most—that you didn't kill him right then for laying his hands on Ally or that you didn't toss him and Alan out the window."

"It was a near thing," he admitted with a nod.

For a long moment, she was silent, studying him. Uncomfortable, he shifted, wondering what she was picking up. With her, he was never sure.

"For good reason," she murmured, her lips quirking into a brief smile. "God knows you kept me on my toes. Still do," she corrected herself. "It's only fair I keep a few tricks up my sleeve."

"When I got your letter about her annulment," JW spoke slowly, "I wondered what you would do if you knew any witch's curses or something."

"Use them on Kevin, of course," Zoey replied easily.

"You think you could turn him into a toad or something?" he suggested with rare whimsy.

"I wish," she sighed, sitting back down. "JW, I haven't often interfered in your personal life."

"I don't think you ever have," he assured her. "Or embarrassed me the way other parents did, which I'm grateful for." Smiling, she put a hand on his thigh and he met her gaze. "But you're about to now, aren't you?"

"Well, you've mucked it up as much as you could on your own," she drawled. "I thought I'd try to help you clean it up."

"I've talked to Liam. Rather, he came up to the cabin and unloaded a shit load on me," he started slowly, not sure what she knew or how she would react.

"Good," she approved.

Sending her a wry look, he continued, "He said everyone who might have been interested has replied that they will not bid. Except Madison."

"Asshole number two to worry about," she muttered.

"Let's focus on this," he suggested, knowing how she could wander down paths of thought. "I can easily outbid him. His businesses have taken severe hits since he first went after Ally in June. His cash flow isn't what it used to be."

"And when the auction is over? What are you going to do with Ally?"

Prepared for her protectiveness toward Ally, JW turned to meet her gaze fully and handed her the small box. Opening it and understanding immediately, Zoey blinked back tears. Throwing her arms around his neck, she kissed his cheek.

"About damned time," she whispered as he hugged her.

"You approve?" he teased.

Her hand smacked the back of his head and he laughed.

"Talk to her, JW. Before you do anything else. Clear the air between you so you can start fresh."

"I will, Mom. I promise. I might be slow at some things, but I do learn."

"That's my boy," she sighed, resting her forehead on his shoulder. "All I have ever wanted is for you to be loved, to be happy. Ally will do that for you. And you for her."

Chapter Eleven

Ally opened her eyes and didn't recognize the ceiling. Rolling to her right, she winced as her memory came back with painful clarity. She'd signed the contract, tried to stand, and passed out. What a lovely first impression to make on her new master.

Logically, Ally knew she was now with her new owner. Taking stock of how her body felt, she was pretty sure he hadn't fucked her while she'd been unconscious. Sitting up, she closed her eyes as the room spun around her. Taking several breaths, she opened her eyes and slowly moved her head to look around.

Frowning, she took in the furnishings. They were rustic, comfortable, and worn from use. The walls resembled the inside of a log cabin. Twisting to the window behind the bed, she separated the curtains and peered out into the darkness. Starlight glittered off the snow, and she realized that she was in a log cabin in the middle of a clearing surrounded by tall trees. That told her absolutely nothing about her new master. Nearly all of the club members could afford a place in the country, and a number of them were into hunting and fishing.

Relief swept her though. She was fairly certain that Madison and a couple others into the extreme edge of the lifestyle rarely left the city, which still left quite a few that she might need to worry about. With a snort, she shook her head. *Madison would have done God knows what to me while I was out of it. And he would have enjoyed it. I can probably be fairly certain that he isn't my new master*. That hope, her pessimist side reminded her, still contained a lot of uncertainties.

"All right," she muttered to herself. "Let's try to be positive about all this and not trip into a panic attack or something."

Glancing at the clock, she realized it was five o'clock. She guessed it must be morning, as she didn't feel like she'd slept for an entire day. Ally's stomach rumbled loudly and cramped as if she hadn't eaten in days. Then again, she hadn't. She'd wanted to punish herself. For Master JW leaving her a second time. For being so stupid as to be with him the second time.

Next to the clock, a piece of paper sat propped up against the lamp on the nightstand. Taking it, she read the handwriting. *Slave, Take a shower and groom yourself completely. Leave the bedroom and kneel facing the fireplace. Put the blindfold on and wait for me. Master*

No clue as to who her master was. Through the open door to the right, she could see the shower and, sliding from the bed, headed off to follow his orders after using the toilet.

She shampooed and conditioned her hair, then carefully shaved her legs, pussy, and armpits. Drying herself, she rubbed the lotion on the counter into her skin and combed her hair. Unable to find a hair dryer, Ally hoped that her new master didn't mind damp hair and left the bathroom.

She paused near the bed. Her mind screamed that this was wrong. Whoever was out there wasn't Master JW. Could never be who she wanted and needed.

I'll punish you in the morning. Ally grabbed the heavy wood post at the foot of the bed. Punish her for what? She hadn't had a chance to do anything! Or had she? Had she said something after she'd passed out? Or had her fainting angered him? Was that why her new master intended to punish her?

Turning to the now open bedroom door, she swallowed. Her master was out there. He could do anything he wanted to her. Given the contract she'd signed, she had no recourse, no way to fight him without exposing the club. That would destroy everyone involved, and she could never do that to David and Diana. Wrapping her arms around her waist, she walked slowly to the door and paused. Taking a deep breath and wishing she hadn't done this, she looked around.

Outside the bedroom, the first floor of the cabin seemed to be one large room with the living and kitchen areas flowing together. The breakfast bar seemed to be the only divider. Beyond its granite surface, she could see a decent-size kitchen with a large island. Closer at hand was the living area. A large plaid upholstered couch faced the hearth, flanked by side tables and two large, oversize chairs with footstools. The only light came from the flames.

Remembering the directions, she moved to her right. A black silk blindfold lay on the edge of the large dark red cushion. That consideration surprised her. Everything she'd heard about slave masters had indicated cages, confinement, and harsh treatment.

A flash of memory forced her to grab the back of the nearby leather chair. The last time, Master JW had bound her to a spanking bench after she'd had several orgasms. Unable to move and helpless, she had still trusted him completely. Could she trust another man like that? She had tried at the club and not been able to. So, what did she do? She had quite easily jumped from the frying pan into the fire.

Ally, you idiot! You should have tried to contact him, asked Master Liam to get a message to him, something, anything besides this. And now, it's too late. Fingers tightening on the leather, she took a deep breath and forced her feet to move. She had done this. She had given her word and she would see it through.

Lowering herself to the cushion, she spread her knees and sat back on her heels. The heat of the fire felt good and for a moment she savored the warmth. Picking up the blindfold, she managed to put it on, hoping her new master would think it secure enough.

Unable to see, she tried to steady her breathing, ears straining to catch the slightest sound that might indicate the presence of her master. Behind the blindfold, tears gathered in her eyes, slipping under the silk to glide down her cheeks.

The heat of the fire suddenly disappeared as he stepped in front of her. His hands gripped her head and pulled her off her heels. Almost immediately, she felt the head of his cock against her lips. Obedient to his implicit command, she opened her mouth and he thrust deep into her wet heat.

"Oh, yes. Good girl."

For a moment, she couldn't move, think, or breathe. Her brain froze at the sound of his voice. *His voice.* He pulled his thick shaft nearly out then forced it back in. She shuddered at the familiar taste of him on her tongue. What the hell *is* going on? When he withdrew again, she reacted instinctively.

Reaching up, she pulled the blindfold off and stared up into green eyes. Not recognizing the wounded cry that came from her own throat, she scrambled backward off the cushion, not stopping until she collided with the couch and collapsed on the floor.

Gasping for air, as stunned as he obviously was by her actions, she waited for him to respond. And drank in the sight of him. Standing in front of the fire, legs apart and hands planted on his hips, with his hard cock jutting out, he looked very much like he'd sprung from the depths of hell. And he was the demon whose touch she craved.

After he explained what the hell was going on.

"You are a bad girl," he said quietly. "A very bad girl."

"Stay away from me," she told him, holding a hand out when he stepped over the cushion. "Just…stay away."

"What are you talking about?" he demanded. "We have a contract."

No, it was more a growl. She could tell he was pissed. Well, fine. She was scared and angry, and she wanted answers.

He was on her before she could blink. His long arms reached down and hauled her up against his taut body. He loomed over her before pressing her to sit on the couch. His left knee landed on the cushion next to her thigh. The foot of his prosthesis planted itself near her left hip.

"I don't understand," Ally whispered pitiably, drawing her legs against her chest.

"What? What don't you understand?" His frustration was obvious even in her shaken state.

"Everything. I don't understand why you kissed me that night in the garden. I don't understand how you affect me the way you do. I don't understand why no one else does. I don't understand why you left me the first time or the second. Or…"

"Stop," he ordered in a calm, controlled voice. She snapped her jaw shut. "I didn't leave you the second time. I went down to the pub. When I came back, *you* were gone."

She stared at him in shock.

"You came back?" she breathed, hope welling in her heart.

"I did," he replied, defensively. "I left my coat on the chair. I couldn't think in the same room with you. If I stayed, I was going to take you again. I had to think clearly. So I left. I came back."

Had his coat been there? She couldn't remember. She'd been so upset about waking up alone. *What was that?*

"You couldn't think clearly around me? What about now? You seem to have recovered your mental facilities."

His right eyebrow quirked up.

"I think while we're having this discussion, we'll ignore the normal protocols."

Catching her breath, Ally frowned.

"No punishments?"

"Before or after you took off the blindfold?" he wondered, a dry tone to his voice.

"Both," she answered quickly. "Please. Just explain things to me. Help me understand you and why…" She looked up and saw the pain in his expression. "I know I won't understand everything you've been through. No one can, except someone who has been in your shoes. My grandfather survived the Battle of the Bulge and my uncle survived Vietnam. Having someone listen can be the biggest help of all. It doesn't block the memories, but it can make them easier to deal with."

Somewhere behind her, something gurgled.

"The coffeemaker," he explained when she tried to see over the back of the couch and the high counter. "I thought you'd sleep longer, and I need to get back onto some sort of schedule."

"Do you need some before we talk?" Ally asked tentatively.

He shook his head.

"I'll give it a minute before I get a cup. Liam said you drink tea. I've got that too. I had no idea what kind you'd like, so I bought one of everything the store had."

"Thank you," she replied, more confused than ever by the man who stood in front of her. "JW, why did you buy my contract? All you had to do was contact me, ask me to withdraw from the auction. And…" she shook her head. "We don't know much about each other."

"You want to talk?"

His tone reminding her of the way they'd batted the words about two weeks earlier.

His semi-erect cock flexed inches from her face. She knew how easy it would be for him to dominate her, pull her under his control. All he had to do was grab her head and push his cock between her lips and down her throat. Despite pulling away before, she knew she wouldn't fight him. She was at the point of she would take whatever he would give her.

"I just want to know why you bought my contract," she replied, feeling more vulnerable than she had that horrible night with Kevin. Recognizing it for the self-protective action it was, she wrapped her arms around her shins. "Why…"

She sighed.

"Because if I'd done the right thing fifteen months ago, so much might have been different. Maybe not for me, but definitely for you."

"What do you mean?" Ally wondered, lifting her chin enough to see his face. She had not been expecting that answer at all. Nor the regret in his voice.

JW stared down at her, frowning.

"We don't know much about each other in some ways," he spoke carefully. "But that night, when I scared your headache away," JW quipped. Ally smiled in spite of herself. "I scared myself. That kiss scared the shit out of me. And I ran."

"A kiss scared you?" She shook her head, having a hard time with that line.

"What did you feel, Ally? Do you remember?" He prompted.

Meeting his gaze, seeing urgency in the green depths, Ally let herself feel that moment again.

"Alive. Wild. Safe," she whispered. "It was magical. Like a light flipped on inside me. Then…" she caught the words in her throat and dropped her chin.

"Then I left you," he finished.

Blinking back tears, she nodded.

"I'm sorry," he said quietly.

Startled, Ally brought her head up again.

"What?" she breathed.

"Of all the things in my life I wish I could change, that's the only one on the list," he told her. "I would have at least asked if you would write me, not go out with anyone else until I could see you again. But instead, I ran. Granted," he tilted his head, "there was a bit more to it than the kiss but—"

"Is that why Nick wanted to talk to you?" Ally asked. His body jerked and she smiled. "Why don't you sit down so I don't get a crick in my neck and you're more comfortable while we talk?"

"Trying to top from the bottom?" he asked archly.

Blushing she shook her head.

"No, sir. I just have a feeling this is going to take a while."

"By the time I finish telling you, you might want something stronger than tea," he warned her.

"You're secretly married to a supermodel and have a half dozen kids?" she guessed, giggling at the shock on his face. "Okay, if it's not anything like that, then I can handle it."

"I'm holding you to that," he replied, shaking his head as he stepped back from the couch. "Go on in the kitchen and fix some tea. I'll get some pants on."

"Don't get dressed on my account," Ally called after him as he moved to the bedroom.

Pausing at the doorway, JW glanced over his shoulder.

"I had no idea you were like this," he commented with a quirk to his mouth.

"Is that good or bad?" she wondered.

"Go get your tea," he smiled, disappearing into the dark bedroom.

Grinning, Ally wrapped a fleece blanket around her shoulders and went to explore his kitchen. Putting the kettle on first and taking two mugs from the iron stand, she opened cabinets to see what was where. Her eyes popped wide when she saw the shelves, plural as in three, full of boxes of tea. Wearing jeans zipped but not buttoned, JW came from the bedroom.

"See anything you like?" he asked with a chuckle.

"All I have to do is make up my mind," she marveled, reaching for her favorite breakfast tea. "Diana has me hooked on this one," she told him, struggling to remove the plastic from the box. Finally successful, she removed a bag and put it in the mug he'd left for her. She watched him move along the counter, feeling a bit more confident in letting her eyes roam his body. "And, I definitely see something I like."

Glancing at her, he winked at her expression.

"That's a good thing, sweetheart."

As he poured his coffee, the aroma hit her nostrils. Blinking she glanced sideways at it. "You like your coffee to be able to climb out of the mug and arm wrestle you?"

"It gets the blood flowing," he smiled as the kettle whistled.

Beverages in hand, they returned to the fireplace. Hesitant, Ally paused by her original cushion.

"Before you start talking," she ventured. "Could you answer a question?"

"As long as it's not classified," he agreed.

"Why did you buy my contract? Please don't tell me it was because you felt guilty. I couldn't bear that."

"Because the thought of another man touching you wasn't to be considered," JW said flatly.

She searched his face in the flickering light.

"Then why…"

"Go through with it?" he wondered, sitting down and sipping his coffee. "Why make you go through the auction? Why bid on you and then make you sign a contract?"

"Yes," she whispered, sitting on the cushion and drinking her tea.

"A contract that you didn't read," JW reminded her. "Which is why you earned a punishment."

Startled, Ally stared at him.

"Liam had gone through it with me," she protested. "He made sure I knew what was in it."

"Masters can make adjustments, add things, subtract things," he commented with a slightly ominous tone.

"What?" She swallowed, then sipped more tea trying to gather her thoughts. After calling her 'sweetheart' in the kitchen, this wasn't what she expected. *Now what is going to happen?* "What adjustments did you make?"

He reached out and took her mug from her, setting it on the table with his. Getting up, he moved to join her, squatting on his haunches next to the cushion.

"I removed all your safeguards."

There was no expression in his voice. No emotion. Her world shifted. Ally couldn't move. Couldn't breathe. *No safeguards?*

"I removed your right to redress the contract to the board."

I'm not hearing this. Trembling, she stared at him. His left hand reached out and cupped the right side of her jaw. His thumb stroked her cheek.

"I made you completely dependent on me."

The pad of his thumb pressed against her lips as he smiled at her. His eyes shone with triumph, of knowing that he controlled her.

"I made myself responsible for everything about you. Where you go. What you can do. What you eat. What you wear." His right hand rested on her left shoulder. The fingers moved over her collarbone, down to her breast to pinch a nipple. She bit her lip but the moan escaped. "Your pleasure and pain."

His hand covered her breast, fingers kneading until she whimpered and her hips shifted.

"I removed things and I added things," he continued in a slow, almost hypnotic voice.

"Added things?" she breathed as his hand shifted to her hip.

"Yes," came his whisper. "The last two pages were rather detailed. It removed and added very explicit details."

"Like what?" she gasped as his hand covered her pussy and rubbed against her dripping folds. His fingers parted her, teasing the hole until she trembled.

The hand at her jaw moved to the back of her neck as he shifted and knelt on the edge of the cushion.

"Look at me, pet," he whispered.

Only then did she realize she had closed her eyes, caught up in the seductive haze of his voice and touch. Green fire blazed in his eyes. Unable and unwilling to look away, she stared back at him. Slowly realizing just how trapped she was, how utterly dependent on him for everything, including her life.

"What are you going to do with me?" she whimpered.

"It was a prenuptial agreement."

Ally stared at him, unable to comprehend, then unable to believe what she'd heard.

"What?" she breathed. "What did you say?"

A smile curved his lips, reached his eyes. The hand at her pussy moved, went to his back pocket then held something before her. Stunned, she stared at the ring. Smiling, he slipped it on her finger.

"My father was killed in a car accident. One of the few things that survived the fire was a ring he'd bought for my mother. It was set with their birthstones," he explained, adjusting the ring. "So, I thought I'd continue that tradition with our birthstones for your ring."

Still struggling to understand, Ally dropped her gaze and looked at the ring that was surrounded by tiny diamonds, pearl for her June birthdate and... She glanced at him.

"Amethyst," he told her. "My birthday's the fourth of February."

"I don't...don't understand," she whispered in confusion.

"I want to make sure that every man alive knows that you're mine," he answered. "I want you to know that you're mine." His hand claimed her pussy. Two fingers plunged inside, making her cry out in need. "Mine, Ally. No one else's."

His mouth covered hers, tongue sweeping inside to tangle and tug on hers. With a moan, she closed her eyes as he coaxed her body's response. Heat flared and flashed through her blood. Her pussy tightened around his stroking fingers. Slowly believing, she put her hands on his biceps, then stroked them over his shoulders to the back of his neck.

Panting, she writhed against him. The callused heel of his hand rubbed her clit.

"Please," she moaned.

"Come on, sweetheart," he coaxed. "Let me hear you."

Fingers threaded in her hair, tightening and pulling her head back. His mouth teased her ear lobe, nibbling as his tongue stroked the sensitive nerves.

"Ah," she gasped, pressing against his muscular torso.

His lips explored the column of her neck, tongue licking and teasing. He guided her upper body back and over his left upper arm. Her breasts thrust up for his pleasure. His mouth captured one nipple, sucking in as much of the soft mound as he could. Her head fell back as her hands clutched his head.

"Please," she begged.

"No need for permission this time," he told her, nibbling his way to the other breast. "I want everything you can give me, baby."

"I want you," she pleaded. "Please. I need you."

"I'm right here, sweetheart. I'm not going anywhere," he assured her, yet with a teasing lilt.

"Inside me," Ally insisted, feeling she'd go mad. "I need you inside me. I need to feel you."

His low chuckle reassured her on several levels. He knew what he was doing to her, wanted it, relished it; yet, he was still in control. Still very much her master.

"Come for me, sweetheart," he commanded now, three fingers filling her pussy.

Closing her eyes, Ally felt the heat in her lower belly build, tightening like a coiled spring. His strength surrounded her. His hands and mouth stroked her body, knowing just where the nerves lay. She writhed against him, relishing the feel of his hard body as covered with light perspiration as hers was. With a growl, his mouth claimed hers, their tongues tangling.

And her body jerked once as if she'd brushed up against an electric wire. As his hand stroked into her again, the fingers in her hair tightened. His mouth ravished and she flew.

With a strangled cry, her mouth tore from his as she arched back. Body stiffening as the orgasm swept through her, Ally saw stars exploding behind closed eyelids. His thumb flicked over her clit and pushed her again with another shriek. Panting for air, she collapsed against his chest.

Reluctantly pulling his hand from her pussy, JW cradled her head to his shoulder, brushing damp strands of hair from her sweaty forehead. He'd been in the living room and heard her waking up. When she'd left the bathroom, he'd started the coffee and waited in the shadows of the kitchen for her to appear. Seeing her slender body, he could see the weight loss of the past days and cursed himself for hurting her. Her reaction when he finally spoke had stunned him, but he took advantage of the opening she'd given him. Taking his mother's advice to talk, he thought he'd made a good start by bringing up the contract she hadn't read before signing and putting the ring on her finger. *That should reassure her on some levels.* Yet, there was definitely more to her and he liked that. She'd loved and lost, been hurt and recovered. She was stronger, but he knew he'd live with the guilt forever for what she'd gone through with Kevin.

And that, he told himself, was the next part of any conversation.

"JW?" she murmured. "Tell me what happens next."

Shifting his weight, he planted his prosthesis on the floor and pushed up, standing with her in his arms. A couple steps back and he sat down in the chair.

"Now, we talk a bit," he replied.

"About what?" Ally put a hand to the side of her head. "My brain is spinning."

He studied her face and smiled.

"What questions are going through your mind?"

"Where to start with that?" she murmured, then glanced at the ring on her finger. "This is real? You really…" Her eyes lifted and he saw the apprehension. "Why?"

"This is going to sound insane because, on many levels we don't know each other," he started, kissing her forehead, "but at the one that counts the most, it's the most sane thing I've ever done."

"JW," she sighed with obvious exasperation.

"I love you," he told her simply. "The connection was so fast, so hard when I saw you, when I heard your voice, when I kissed you," he shook his head. "It scared me. I've heard people talk about it, about the connection, but no one ever told me that it rocked your world like that. It turned me inside out."

"You make it sound like loving me is a bad thing," she whispered.

"Not a bad thing at all," he smiled, squeezing his arms. "But terrifying for a man who was sure he'd never feel the emotion."

"What do you mean by 'connection'?" Ally frowned.

JW paused.

"Where to start on that?"

"The beginning," she deadpanned.

He snorted.

"I'm not sure there is one."

"Pick a spot then, but start somewhere," Ally frowned with impatience.

"Topping from the bottom again?"

"No," she shook her head. "But a submissive, slave, pet, whatever, is still able to be strong. And you'd be bored with a limp noodle in or out of bed."

Chuckling, JW gave her a hard kiss that left her breathless.

"True," he agreed. He handed her the tea then took a healthy swallow of coffee. "In 1823, Padraig O'Grady landed in New York City straight from Ireland. An English lord had threatened him for defending his sister's honor. So, with his sister in tow, he set out for America. He started working in the pub of another Irishman who loved the drink more than he should have, and within a couple years, had bought the man out. Padraig's son added a hotel to the pub, which had become rather fancy by the time of the Civil War. Padraig's grandson added on to it again, starting what he called the Shadows."

"The club," she murmured. "So, Liam continues the tradition."

"He does," JW confirmed. "And there's another inheritance for Padraig's descendants. One not known to those outside the family or close circle of friends." He lifted the mug again. "Padraig claimed he was the seventh son of a druid. He had visions, could tell if a man was lying, what a person was feeling…"

"Nick," she breathed.

"Excuse me?" he frowned at her interruption.

"That night in the garden," Ally whispered. "He said he'd felt the people in the Twin Towers. Their fears. Their pain. He mentioned Giselle and…"

"My mother," he finished.

"Oh, my God," Ally swallowed. "I can't imagine what that must have felt like. How horrible for them! How did they manage to deal with it?"

For a moment, JW could only stare at her acceptance and immediate concern for his cousins and mother. Slowly, he smiled and the tightness he'd carried for so long began to ease.

"Mom gave Giselle something to sedate her. Nick was in school in Connecticut and broke into the headmaster's house to steal a couple bottles of brandy."

"The poor boy," Ally whispered. "How bad was his hangover?"

"He drank nearly all of it and had barely recovered when I arrived Friday afternoon," JW told her.

"And your mother? What did she feel? What did she do?" JW blinked.

"I don't know," he admitted. "Knowing Mom, she probably focused on absorbing whatever Gisele's pain and trying to stay calm."

"She felt it too, then?" Ally persisted.

"She did, but Gisele is a stronger empath.," JW replied, realizing that the one time he'd asked her about it, upon his arrival days later, his mother had sidestepped the question.

"Calm," Ally echoed. "When we met that night, she called me a center of calm, that she would stay close to me."

He considered that, recalling Grant's comments before he'd left the hospital, and slowly nodded.

"She's right," he reflected. "I felt it when you touched my arm. I felt calmer, balanced. Mom's the only one who's made me feel that." He studied her. "You have anything to say about that?"

She shook her head.

"I've always been a bit weird. I never really fit into the cliques in school, but I got along with everyone."

"What about your family? Anyone ever mention odd things in the family tree?"

Frowning, she thought about it. JW liked how relaxed she was in his arms, resting her head against his shoulder.

"Grandpa Mack said an aunt was a bit 'off'," she finally said. "That she would go off into the woods, collecting berries or leaves or something. There were some jokes she was a witch." She shrugged. "Not much else. He never really talked about his family no matter how much I asked him questions."

"Well, that's something we can dig into if you'd like," he suggested.

With a quick smile, she nodded.

"And what about you?" she asked him. "What gift of Padraig's druid did you inherit? Besides," she stretched up to whisper in her ear, "the ability to kiss a woman senseless?"

At her breathy voice, JW felt his body respond. His cock was quickly ready to remind her who her master was.

"I'm a bit of an empath," he admitted. "Nothing close to Giselle or even Mom or Nick."

"What about Nora?" Ally wondered. "She has green eyes too."

He smiled at her attention to detail.

"You caught that, did you?"

"Everyone else has brown or blue eyes," she said. "Except you, your mom, Giselle, Nick, and Nora." Her own eyes widened. "And Liam and Seamus."

"It's one reason Liam is so good at his job," JW quipped with a grin, then sighed. "We're not sure about Nora's ability or strength.

She's only thirteen and hasn't felt it yet." He shrugged. "At least not that she or anyone else have told me about."

"How old were you when you realized you had a gift? And what is yours?" Curiosity filled her voice.

"I was thirteen. It usually waits for puberty to hit. Like the hormones teens are feeling aren't enough of a problem," he drawled. Ally smiled and settled back in his arms. "I can pick up emotions if they're strong. Feel things happening in relatives. And see things."

His voice drifted off as he recalled the vision he'd had when he'd first kissed her.

"What? What did you see?" she was quick to read his expression.

"That night in the garden," JW whispered. "I saw the explosion that took my leg. I felt it. And saw my body landing on the rocks."

With a gasp, she wrapped her arms around him.

"You're here with me," she told him, an unexpected fierceness in her voice. "You're here with me."

Holding her tight, he took a deep breath.

"I have nightmares."

"I know," she replied. "You had one the first time at the club."

JW groaned.

"I did? What about?"

"I think it was probably classified," she told him with an impish expression. "So, I probably shouldn't discuss it with you."

He laughed, relaxing a bit more with her.

"And that was before things got interesting," he murmured.

"Tell me about JW Franklin. Who you are," she urged. "Just a little."

"Not much to tell," he shrugged. "Let's see. I went to the schools I was expected to, all the boarding school stuff. I did the sports. I enlisted right out of high school. I couldn't stand the thought of college or going into business the way Grandfather wanted all of us to. Sitting in an office for hours on end? No way, thank you very much. After Basic, I went through Special Forces training. My shooting was good, so I became a sniper. I deployed for Operations Desert Shield and Storm, a few missions after, and then 9/11 happened."

"Where were you when the Towers went down?" she wondered.

"Out in the middle of nowhere in Texas on an exercise." He smirked. "I had just bagged a major general, two full birds, and a major."

"Making an impression," she murmured.

"That's about what Mom said," he told her.

"I don't understand people who can do things like what happened that day," Ally whispered. "Or since. Thousands of people killed. They got up and went to work or school." Tears filled her eyes. "And never went home."

"Innocents," he stated.

"Yes," she agreed with a nod, eyes on his expression. "You left almost immediately, didn't you? Right after that party? That's why your family was tense. You went straight to Afghanistan. To hunt down the people who planned it."

His eyes narrowed.

"Ally, that is *so* classified."

"Operational security and stuff," she nodded, accepting his non-answer. "Grandpa Mack and Uncle Jack talked about it. But, well…" she bit her bottom lip. "Can you tell me if you got some of the ones who did it? Some of the ones who planned it? Who followed them?"

Ally could see the appreciation in his eyes. The realization that she understood and wanted some sort of justice for all the lives lost. And the caution in his voice told her more.

"There are fewer of them now because of what our teams did."

"Good," she replied with a nod. "I wish you hadn't had to go, but I'm glad you did." She closed her eyes and cringed. "I know that sounds horrible, but I…" She exhaled. "I'm sorry. I interrupted and sidetracked you."

"It's all right." His voice was low, as if remembering things he'd done, people he'd known, and she hoped he realized that they had more in common than a hunger for rough sex. More than just this insatiable lust for each other.

The only sounds came from the crackling fire and soft ticking of the grandfather clock behind her. It was as if the rest of the world disappeared.

"What happened, JW?" she whispered. "The last time you were there."

"I'm sure you've read all the stories about it," he shrugged nonchalantly.

"Like I'm going to believe anything the newspapers say?" she retorted. "After some of what they printed about me?"

"Which was?" he frowned. "What do you mean? Why would they have been writing about you?"

"After your story," she replied, with a grin.

JW considered her.

"You have gotten stronger," he commented. "I can see it in your eyes."

"Remember that."

His arms held her securely to his chest. Smiling to herself, she rested her head on his shoulder and relaxed.

"Tell me, JW," she softly ordered. "Just once. Tell me everything that happened when you went after Ben Hancock."

"Jesus, Ally," he groaned. "I didn't even tell those damned therapists at Walter Reed." He referred to the military hospital outside DC. "Not beyond what we each told for the official report."

"I majored in American history, but minored in psychiatry. I wanted to better understand what my grandfather and uncle went through. Not to mention all the books I've read the past year or so."

He frowned down at her.

"So you're a therapist?"

She laughed.

"Hardly, but I do know it helps. Just tell me once. Everything. The good, the bad, and the ugly."

"I can't do that."

Ally tilted her head.

"Browns are stubborn creatures, JW. I won't give up on you. Ever."

For a long moment, he didn't respond. She stayed quiet, eyes on his face.

"Parker, he's my spotter, and I were farther down the valley when we heard the gunfire. There was a brief spurt on the radio and we recognized the voice as a sergeant serving with Ben. We were already running as fast as we could. We reached the front of the line first as the Taliban started to pull back. The lieutenant, Will Adams, said Ben and three others were to the rear. Parker and I went with Quincy. Two of the men were dead. Corporal Stevens told us they'd taken Ben. That the Taliban had been looking for him specifically. For ransom or to showcase the evils of America."

Ally pressed her cheek against his chest, arms tightening slightly. His hand stroked her hair.

"Helicopters finally came for the wounded and dead," he whispered. "Adams was trying to get permission to go after Ben. The command said they'd take it under *advisement* and pass it up the chain," came his sneer. "Stevens grabbed Adams' hand, repeating what he'd told us when we found him. That the Taliban had been looking for Ben. He had been their target." JW shook his head. "The colonel at the other end didn't care. He ordered us all back to the FOB."

"FOB?" Ally whispered.

"Forward operating base," he explained. "We stood there as the last of the wounded were air lifted out. If we went back to the FOB, Ben was a dead man. Adams switched the radio off. He said we could leave if we wanted, but he was going after the captain. I nodded and said let's go. Quincy, who's half Sioux, just turned and went back to where Ben had been taken and found their tracks."

"How many of you?"

"Twelve of us went," JW answered. "They had a four-hour head start on us and knew the land." He smiled. "But we had Quincy. I swear that man talked to the birds a few times to figure out which way they'd gone. Birds or the rocks. Rain flooded a stream and forced us to stop for a few hours and we were really worried. They'd be doing God knew what to Ben, and we were cut off until the water went down. As soon as the rain slowed up a little, we went looking for a way to cross. Parker found a downed tree and we used it."

He closed his eyes, his arm tightening around her.

"They reached their village hideout eighteen hours before we caught up to them. They whipped him publicly. Encouraged boys to throw stones at him, and then they got serious about torture and asking questions."

Ally closed her eyes and turned her face against his shoulder.

"He told me when we were stateside again that he answered with Bible quotes. Every time they hit him, he yelled 'hallelujah' or 'amen'."

"Remarkable," she murmured, trembling against him.

"We finally reached the village. A boy saw us and took off toward the house, yelling that the Americans were coming, kill the infidel."

"Oh, my God," Ally breathed, realizing how tight the timing must have been.

"That boy took us straight to them. Not really a boy, I guess," he murmured. "Closer to mid-teens. Someone, I don't know who, killed him. I saw his body outside the compound. Adams, Quincy, and I fought our way to the second floor. Quincy shot the lock and Adams and I went in. They were filming, getting ready to behead him. Adams, God bless him, didn't hesitate. His arm came up and he fired, shooting the man holding the sword over Ben's head. Best damn shooting I've ever seen. I killed the other three."

"Oh, my God," she whispered, shaking but unable to take her eyes from his face. *He's reliving all of it now. Please, God, please let this help him a little.*

"Quincy stayed in the hallway covering our backs. Adams and I ran to Ben, cut his ropes, and dragged him out. We gathered up the Taliban weapons and ammunition and fought our way out of the village. I have no idea how many we killed. And I honestly don't care. We didn't have time for anything but getting as far as we

239

could. Later, we realized that, while we'd gone in looking for Ben, some Taliban had set up an ambush along the way we'd come. They set up a tripwire. Thompson was on point and didn't see it. I was about three paces behind him when it blew him to pieces and nearly took me with him."

Holding her trembling body, JW let the memory of the explosion flood his mind and body. It had been just like the image that had flashed before his eyes before he'd first kissed Ally. As the explosion rang in his ears, his body crashing into the rocks, it had been that embrace in his thoughts. The need for her, the regret of not doing something. Burying his face against her hair, he realized he'd compounded that mistake by not asking for her as soon as he woke up and was aware of his surroundings. Her strength had always been there but the past year, she'd discovered it for herself and grown stronger. And now she gave it to him. *I don't deserve her but, God help me, I'm not letting her go.*

"I thought of you," he told her now. "That kiss. I held onto that." Her fingers moved slightly against his chest. "A patrol heard the explosion and firefight and called in support. As fast as that chopper came though, the medics wouldn't have been able to do anything to save my leg or Adams' eye. But they kept more of us from dying, from bleeding to death. I was kept sedated most of the time. I remember my mom being there at one point. Probably in Germany. Then I saw Ben at Reed. He came in on crutches and he told me some general was trying to have us all court-martialed, but

Mom, Grandmother, and his grandmother were pushing back at the Pentagon. They called in every political favor the families were owed. Mom came in and then…" he swallowed. "Then I saw my leg, or rather the lack of it. I broke down. I just held onto Mom and cried like a wuss."

"No," she protested swiftly, lifting her head and glaring at him.

"I suppose you're going to say it was a natural reaction to the shock of the loss," he drawled.

"That and being safe," she replied, lifting her hand to cradle his jaw. "After what you and the men accomplished, to be told some asshole wanted to court-martial you, and then see you'd lost your leg below the knee? To have your mother there? The one person you knew was hurting with you?" Her brown eyes filled with tears. "JW, I would be astonished if you hadn't cried."

"I didn't cry," he corrected. "I sobbed like a baby."

"Would it have changed anything?" She frowned, eyes narrowed. "JW, if you'd known what would happen to you personally or what the Army would try to do to all of you, would you still have gone after Ben?"

A smile curved his mouth and he kissed her quickly.

"That's pretty much what Mom said a few days later."

"Your mother is a brilliant, astute woman," she deduced with a smile.

"That she is," JW agreed, relaxing slightly.

Ally was quiet in his arms. He felt her calm and strength seep into him much as his mother would give him. Except Ally did it without knowing.

"Now I don't know what the fuck to do."

"My grandfather said that getting up every morning was a victory over his enemies," she said quietly. "And his demons."

"Did he talk to you about any of it? Or your uncle?"

"Not until I started college. They thought I was too young, and Mom didn't want them to. Every time she thought they'd talked to me, she got mad at them, as much because they were talking to me as because they wouldn't talk to her. Especially when Uncle Jack said something I'd learned in class helped him." She sighed. "Ma was very protective of me, particularly after Dad died." A sudden giggle came from her. "I can imagine her reaction to the Shadows or some of the things I've done this past year."

"Time to talk about Kevin," he stated firmly.

"No," she whispered. "I can't go there."

"Ally, we're getting everything out now. I'm willing to bet it helps you the way it just helped me." He paused. "I know a bit about him. He was a few years behind me at the school we all went to. I had just gone to my first training course when he and some other punks beat up a scholarship student. They nearly killed him. I can only imagine what he did to you in six weeks. I told you. You tell me."

She tilted her head to meet his gaze.

"Kevin was…" she shook her head. "I didn't understand then. When I couldn't respond to him sexually, he…" She swallowed and put her head back on his shoulder. "He said it was my fault. That I wasn't a real woman. Everything that went wrong in his life ended up being my fault. Pretty much like what I said in the conference room—traffic, bad coffee, and five second erections. He said I was frigid. I didn't orgasm once with him."

JW growled at the insult. *Well, I think we've made up for that.*

"Then David decided not to go in on the Sumatra project with him. I came back to the apartment and…" Her body shuddered, stiffening at the memory. Now, just as JW had, she relived her nightmare. "He dragged me to the bedroom, tied me to the bed, and raped me every way possible. He…he put things in me. I don't know what they were." Which was a lie. She remembered everything— every word, every lash from his belt, every object he'd used. Given how JW had reacted during the meeting, she wasn't about to tell him. "I don't know how many times, but when he was done, he put a bathrobe on me and sent me down to a waiting taxi to take me to David and Diana."

"Holy fuck," JW breathed. "Why didn't you press charges? Why the hell wasn't he arrested?"

"Marital rape isn't recognized as a crime in the *great* state of New York," she sneered.

"And David? What did he say when you showed up on his doorstep?"

243

That worried him. He'd noticed some tension from her, and definitely something from David that he hadn't been able to put his finger on.

"That he'd warned me about Kevin and I should have listened to him."

"Shit. No wonder he was ready to kill him in the conference room," muttered JW. "He felt guilty as shit and wasn't going to let him hurt you again."

"Yeah," Ally nodded.

"Mom and Giselle have told me a little bit of what Kevin said at the Christmas parties. That David had to be held back by Grant, Bron and others."

"I think that was as much the guilt as he was realizing more of what Kevin had done to me," she mused.

"But he didn't ask you then? Or since?" JW didn't like that. *What the hell, David?*

"No," whispered Ally. "Part of me wishes he would, but part of me also understands that some things a woman might go through are extremely difficult for the men who care about her to hear. Something about the alpha complex, men protecting women since caveman days and all that."

"Yeah, it wasn't easy for me to ask and hear you answer," he replied quietly.

"Needless to say, my confidence and sexuality were shredded by the time it was annulled and the holiday parties were over. David insisted I go to therapy, mental as well as finish the physical. When the car crashed that day, killing my family," she whispered, wishing desperately that she could remember, "both my legs were broken, along with four left ribs, my left forearm, and I had a concussion."

"You hit the side of the car?" he guessed.

"I did," she confirmed. "I was unconscious for four days, woke up and wham, bam, I find out I've lost my family and have a cousin. The casts were all taken off on the fourth of September. I was still wobbly when—" Now she swallowed hard at memories. "I felt the impact of the first plane hitting, then heard the explosion. I thought it was a dream about the accident. I finally got out of bed to look out the window and saw the Tower. I yelled for David and Diana."

"Sh," he murmured, hand still moving on her hair.

"David insisted we all evacuate immediately. Robinson took us in the car. Carla came with us and we picked up her son. David stayed to call his people and get them out. He met up with your grandfather and a few others in your family. Robinson met them where cars had to wait for anyone leaving Manhattan. Then I met you." She lightly slapped his chest. "And you left me for the first time. I met Kevin and, by January, after six months of living in the city, I didn't know which end was up. Therapy made sense. After a couple months, Tim suggested I was ready for sexual therapy, which David and Diana would be able to direct me to. And David took me to the Shadows."

"Did it work?" he asked.

Startled out of her reverie, she considered her answer and remembered what he'd said. This was the moment to talk. To tell him everything.

"Only with you." Surprise showed in his face and she smiled. "I trusted you without question. I realized later that that was the problem with Kevin. I didn't trust him. With you," she looked up at him, "I didn't even think about my safe word that first time. I wanted you to do whatever you wanted with me." She bit her lip and looked away as she remembered their first encounter. "I felt like a failure when you left me. Master Liam said you were pleased with me, but still…" Her voice trailed off. "When Dr. Dare cleared me for the selection room, Madison took me. He wouldn't listen when I said no and dragged me out. The other submissives yelled and went after him, even as he was punching me."

"Liam said he put you on demonstrations," JW said quietly.

"He did," she confirmed. "And he tried to have Madison kicked out."

"He alluded to that," JW nodded, eyes on her face.

"The only ones on the board who took his side were his father and your mother," Ally spoke slowly, meeting his gaze.

"Mother knows," he breathed. "Dear God."

"I was embarrassed to look at her in the conference room," Ally admitted. "I was picked in the selection room twice more, but I just didn't feel the same connection I had with you. I used my safe word with each of them. Master Liam decided it was best to use me for classes and demonstrations."

"With no fucking allowed," JW added.

That startled her.

"I didn't know that," she admitted. "I asked him about you. He…he told me about you going after Ben Hancock. About being injured. I wanted to go to you so badly but I didn't know who to talk to so I could see you. David refused to talk about the Shadows once I was in there. Explaining it to your mother or especially Gisele would have been more than a bit awkward. But I wanted to," she whispered. "Oh, I wanted to be with you."

His eyes bore into hers and she could hardly breathe.

"If I'd only stayed with you that night," he whispered. "If I hadn't left you on the bench." His arms tightened around her. "If we'd talked, if I'd asked you to write—"

"I would have," Ally told him earnestly. "Every day. I know you wouldn't have been able to write back as much, or tell me what you were doing, but I would have."

He kissed her forehead.

"Can I add something to the contracts?" she murmured, her hands smoothing over his pecs as she kissed the base of his throat.

"What's that?"

"At least once a week, I get to stroke you, touch you. I know that's more vanilla than submissive, but it's something I need. I need to be able to touch my man." She met his gaze. "I need that."

"Once a week?" he repeated as her hands continued wandering his torso.

"At least," she confirmed, stretching up as a hand tugged his head down, closer to her mouth. "Please."

Chapter Twelve

Shifting around on his lap, Ally took his silence for permission, or at least a show me what you've got. She knew she was breaking all sorts of rules and protocols, but he hadn't put them back in place. Facing him on his thighs, she released the fleece from her shoulders and focused on him. Pressing her breasts to his chest, she nibbled and licked her way up his neck. Her tongue curled and teased his ears. His body shuddered against hers and she smiled as his hands gripped her hips, holding her to his groin.

"You like that?" she wondered, her tongue tracing the edge before she kissed his temple.

"You're making an excellent case," he managed, sounding slightly breathless.

"Let me continue then," Ally murmured.

"You realize you could push me over the edge, don't you? Into losing control?" JW warned.

Leaning back slightly, she smiled at him, then dipped her head to kiss the other side of his neck. "I'm counting on it," she purred.

Fingers tightening on her hips, JW leaned back in the chair, savoring her caresses. No, it wasn't normal, but he enjoyed the idea of her wanting to pleasure him, to explore his body the way he did hers. To know his woman enjoyed him made him want to stand up and roar, fists beating his chest. He closed his eyes.

Her hands stroked his upper body, even as her clever mouth teased hypersensitive nerves. Then she shifted again, moving to get off his lap. Guessing her intent, he caught her waist and opened his eyes.

"What do you think you're doing?" he wondered.

"Continuing my exploration," she replied, her fingers working his zipper down and pushing the denim out of the way.

As she wrapped them around his eager cock, JW groaned.

"Ally."

"Mm?" she wondered, nuzzling the base of his neck.

"Get on the cushion. Like I told you to in the note. Now."

Her head lifted. The expression in his eyes must have told her something because she wasted no time scrambling off his lap. Even as he stood, she was kneeling, reaching for the blindfold, and pulling it on. She sat back on her heels, hands palm up on her knees, waiting for him. Carefully, silently as he had before, he walked to stand between her and the hearth.

His hands caught her head, lifting her off her heels. Automatically, like a baby bird waiting for food, her mouth opened. Smiling, he brushed his thumb over her lips.

"If you come without permission, I'll spank you."

"I'll try to be good, master," she whispered.

He snorted and she smiled as he pushed his cock into her mouth. Closing her eyes, she relaxed. Her master would take care of her just as she would take care of him. The thick erection filled her throat and then he pulled back until she felt the salty precum leaking on her tongue. A few more strokes and she could feel him shuddering as he withdrew completely.

"All fours," he ordered roughly. "Hold onto the edge of the cushion. I'm going to fuck you hard."

She was already obeying as he moved around her. The cushion near her left shin depressed and she heard the firm thud of his right foot. His hands gripped her hips and she lowered her head, bracing herself. The possession was fast and deep. Her body trembled.

"Master," Ally moaned in her need.

"Mine," growled JW.

He pounded in and out of her, as far in as he could, then nearly out of her. The strokes as swift and intense as a jackhammer. Unable to do anything but accept his power over her body, Ally lost herself to the sensations. Her body was being used in the most base ways by a man striving to dominate and control her. By a man whose foremost thought and concern is her. And she relished it. Ally exulted that she could drive this oh-so-disciplined man to the lowest denominator of the human race—the instinctive need to fuck.

Her pussy walls tried desperately to grip the cock that intruded repeatedly. But they were too slick. Perspiration dripped from her skin as lust coiled in her belly.

"Master!"

"Come for me, slave," he ordered in a low husky voice.

His command was a match to kerosene. Her body curled forward, muscles tightening for the tiniest of nudges. A finger brushed her clit and the orgasm exploded through her veins. With a strangled cry, she reared up from the cushion as her pussy seized his cock, finally holding it within. His arms caught her, hands covering her breasts. And his release surged into her, pulsing more heat. With a gasp, her body shuddered again and collapsed against him.

"Oh, my God," she panted. "Oh. Oh."

His fingers pinched her clit and she passed out as a third orgasm pushed her into darkness.

Holding her sweaty, satiated body, JW rested his cheek along her face, closing his eyes. For a long moment, he was content to stay that way

"You've no idea how much I love you," he whispered. "Or what I'll do to protect you."

An exhausted sigh came from her and he smiled, kissing her temple.

"Bed," he decided. "Coffee, tea, and schedules be damned."

****

This time when she woke up, she lay in his arms. With a contented smile, she opened her eyes to see his face, his gaze on hers.

"We made it to the bed," Ally murmured, cuddling against him. "One of these times, you need to make sure I'm awake when you carry me."

"But it's so enjoyable to know I exhausted you that much," he teased, brushing hair back from her cheek.

"Mm," she agreed, stretching and wriggling her hips against his semi-erect cock. "And you do it so well."

"I aim to please," JW told her.

Her head on his bicep, she gazed at his strong features and smiled.

"So now what?"

"As far as?" he wondered.

"Life in general and us specifically."

"Well, I'd never thought of having a big social wedding or anything," he started then frowned. "Okay, to be completely honest, I never thought about getting married period. Whether I would or wouldn't. But, since this is the first for both of us," when she opened her mouth, he put two fingers on her lips, "that was annulled. Remember?" He winked. "Therefore, it legally never happened."

Giggling, she nodded, kissing the fingers.

"I still wouldn't want a big wedding," she told him. "Just David and Diana, your family, maybe a few friends."

"My family," he echoed dryly. "That alone would make it big."

"I don't want to wait until June or whenever we'd have to have it to get everything done."

"Probably a good idea," JW agreed with a nod.

Something in his voice alerted her. Ally pushed up on her right elbow and frowned down at him.

"Do you know something I don't?"

He grinned up at her. "When you and Liam agreed to end your contract, tell me what you did."

"What I did?" she repeated. "Not much. I didn't have clothes or much in the way of personal items, so there was nothing to pack. I'd gone to see Liam, explained why I thought it made sense for me to go back into the real world. Although I told him I'd come back and do demonstrations if he needed me. He argued a little but didn't push too hard, and agreed."

"What else?"

Her brow furrowed as she thought back to that day.

"He called Dr. Dare for an exam, similar to when I'd signed the contract. Blood work. An internal exam. And…" she paused in shock, her jaw dropping open. "He took out the birth control implant in my arm."

"He took out the birth control implant," JW confirmed.

"And my body was back on cycle in two weeks," she breathed, flipping through a mental calendar. "Oh, my God." She looked at him. "JW, there's a very good chance I got pregnant two weeks ago."

"Is that something you would want?" There was gentleness and hope in his question.

Tears filled her eyes as she nodded.

"Very much," she told him. "I want children. I want *your* children. Do you?"

His fingers stroked her cheek before cupping her jaw and pulling her down on top of his chest.

"That's in the prenup as well," he answered. "That you have my children." He rolled them over so she was spread under him. "And no other man's."

She grinned up at him.

"I can definitely promise you that." She rolled her hips against him. "So, um, just in case…"

"In case what?" he smiled.

"In case I'm not already pregnant," she smiled. "I think we should keep trying, just to be sure."

"And when you are," he murmured, kissing her forehead. "We'll figure things out, because I'm fairly certain you'll still be earning punishments."

"Me?" she whispered, eyes wide with innocence. "I'll be as good as gold."

"Really?" he smiled down at her.

"*Weeelll*," she drew it out, then giggled, fingers tickling at his ribs. "Not *too* good. Your spankings get me extra hot inside."

Chuckling, he rubbed his cock along her pussy folds. Closing her eyes, Ally moaned. His upper body lifted. His hands guided her arms over her head. Feeling the rails, she gripped them without being told.

"Is that the only thing that gets you hot inside?" he wondered.

"No, master," she replied, careful not to move as his mouth whispered in her ear.

"No, it's not," he agreed. "You like being helpless. Unable to move. Don't you?"

"Yes, master."

Already, her pussy clenched at a phantom cock, desperate for what only he could give her. He reached over, opening a drawer in the nightstand. Her wrists were bound, then the soft rope tied to the rail. She was blindfolded. His fingers pinched and tugged at her nipples until they were hard peaks and she cried out in her heated need. Clamps were carefully placed around the tips, keeping her on the edge. Then she heard a soft hum and caught her breath.

"You remember me using this on you?" he whispered, teasing her clit and pussy folds with the dildo. "Telling you not to come until I gave you permission."

"Yes, Master," she answered, trembling in need.

"What happened, pet?"

"I came."

"You did," he agreed. "Let's see if you can be a good girl this time."

"I'll try, Master. I really will," she whispered.

In answer, he chuckled. Beneath the silk, she closed her eyes. She might last longer, but he would push her to orgasm without permission. She would simply try to hold on as long as she could. That would please him.

JW smiled, loving how she twisted on the bed, trying so hard to be a good girl. Not much longer, he thought, rubbing the dildo, now nearly as wet as her dripping pussy, against her clit. With a keening cry, she arched up.

"Master, please," she begged. "Please."

He slid the hard toy inside her, imagined her walls gripping it, trying to keep it inside. Pulling it out, he teased her clit again. *Close. Close.* He could hear it in her breathing, the way her body trembled. And he wanted to be inside her.

After, he told himself. He wanted to focus on her. Make her come no matter how hard she tried to hold back.

Ally's breath hitched. A low moan came from her throat. JW pressed her clit, then just to the left and...

He'd hit the spot and put just the right amount of pressure and the orgasm flashed through her. Fingers tightening on the ropes as if to fight it back, she screamed her pleasure, nearly her entire body coming off the mattress. Collapsing back, she panted for air.

The humming stopped and she waited. Would he be pleased? Disappointed?

His mouth covered hers, tongues tangling in their own mating dance. His engorged cock moved over her thigh, paused at her folds, then pushed in. Eagerly, she pulled her knees up as if trying to give him more room.

"Mine," he breathed in her ear. "My sweet submissive."

Beneath the silk, Ally's eyes watered as her master fucked her into exhaustion.

Chapter Thirteen

"I know we have to," she prefaced. "And that we have to deal with the rest of the world, but does it really have to be now? I mean, can't we have a few days or weeks to ourselves?"

Turning from the dresser, JW gave her an indulgent look and she put a pleading expression on her face. He shook his head and she sighed.

"We get everything taken care of now," he told her, putting the wallet in his back pocket before adjusting his watch. "See your family, then we all go to my family and get details hammered out. We'll be back here in three days. Four, tops. A few days at Christmas," he chuckled at her pout. "Don't you want to see Matt on Christmas?"

"Yeah," she agreed with a smile. Getting off the bed, she moved to him and savored the feel of his strong arms around her. "He was only three and a half months old last year. He loved the lights though, especially when David made the them all blink."

"And possibly, this time next year," JW murmured.

Ally could hear the hope in his voice, along with a slight astonishment that he had that hope.

"This time next year, our own baby will be watching his or her daddy play with the lights," she finished.

"I was also thinking," he continued, his hand caressing her back. "We could plan on getting married Christmas Eve. Celebrate that with our families and then, the day after Christmas, fly down to the island ahead of everyone else for a few days of peace and quiet."

"Peace and quiet?" Ally echoed, tilting her head slightly as a smile played about her lips.

"That's what we'll tell everyone else," he grinned wickedly. "The truth will be fucking and resting, resting and fucking until they get down there and we have to act like civilized people."

"Much better," she approved, going up on her toes to brush a kiss across his lips. "Okay. You've convinced me."

"Oh, really?" he drawled.

Biting her bottom lip, she gave him a sideways glance.

"I'm going to be racking up the punishments, aren't I?"

"As always," he confirmed, guiding her out of the bedroom. "How do you think David would react if I asked to borrow his playroom so I could spank you?"

Laughter sputtered out of her as she tried to put her arms in the sleeves of the coat he held for her.

"No, seriously," he told her.

"That about would be his reaction," she laughed, managing the sleeves and buttoning as he reached for his jacket. "As soon as I signed the contract, David was very…" Trying to find the right words, Ally frowned as JW checked that he'd locked back door. "The relationship shifted. I didn't quite understand why or how. We were still working on building one as cousins."

"He's a Dom and you were an unclaimed submissive," explained JW, rejoining her and opening the door. "It doesn't matter if you're his cousin. Although after he and Diana saw you, they went to Liam. Liam said David was livid."

The freezing air had her gasping in shock.

"In the spring," she panted, as he held her close and they descended the stairs and the walk he had carefully shoveled and salted the couple dozen yards to the garage. Shivering, she was glad he'd already raised the garage door. "Could I suggest we build an enclosure or something to the garage? Along with the addition for your office and workout room?"

"Good idea," he nodded.

The ride to the Brown family mansion flew by as they talked. Ally was most interested in the Franklin Christmas traditions and how they could blend them. Having found a legal pad on the old desk in the corner, she made several lists, including one for presents.

"We're going shopping?" he asked, wincing at the thought.

"It's Christmas, JW," she reminded him.

"That's the main reason I try to avoid shopping this time of year," he told her, stopping at the light. "Crowds, idiots in crowds, traffic carrying crowds of idiots. Idiots. Crowds. Did I mention crowds? Or idiots?"

He loved the way her eyes lit up and laughter bubbled out of her.

"You don't like crowds?" she teased.

"Or crowds of idiots," he clarified.

She just giggled, relaxing against the seat, the pad and pen on her lap. Looking around at the decoration on the streetlamps and shops, she smiled.

"We'll get our own tree, won't we?"

"And lights," he promised. "And whatever else you want to put on it. Is there anything in Maine you want to get? To put on the tree?"

Ally's breath caught in her chest and she blinked back tears.

"What?" Concern filled his voice as his hand covered hers on her thigh. "Sweetheart?"

"No one thought of that last year," she whispered. "Understandable, really. After the attacks. My disaster of a first marriage."

"Which didn't happen," he reminded her, squeezing her hand.

"Right," she nodded. "After the attacks," she amended.

"Better," he approved.

"To be honest with you, I don't remember much about Christmas," she confessed.

"Gisele said she went to see you Christmas Eve."

"She did?" Surprised, Ally turned her head to see his face.

"She said you hit David's liquor cabinet. Hard."

Ally winced.

"Yeah, I did. He tried to lock it, but I broke into it on New Year's Eve. A couple days later, he said enough was enough."

"And since?" he wondered.

"I think I've had maybe a glass or two of wine," she replied, trying to recall just when she had. "And even then, I just sipped at it. I never finished the glass, which," she shifted turning her body to face him, "is a good thing when you're trying to get pregnant."

"A very good thing," he smiled, bringing her hand up and kissing her knuckles. "We need to add books on that to your shopping list."

"I already did," she told him with a bright grin.

"That's my girl," he murmured, turning into the drive.

Before they stopped at the bottom of the steps, the right half of the double doors opened. David took them two at a time as Diana appeared behind him with Matt in her arms. Her cousin opened the door as she undid the seat belt and pulled her out.

"Oh, thank God," he breathed, holding her close. "You're here. You're safe and here."

Stunned, she put her arms around him as JW came around the front of the vehicle.

"David, what—"

"A year ago," was all he got out before snapping his jaw shut.

The memory hit her and she stared at him.

"A year ago," she whispered.

A year ago, Kevin happened.

"A year ago," David managed to continue with a nod. "I knew better. I should have told you what Kevin was like. What he's done in the past. I was an arrogant asshole who thought just because

I told you not to do something you would obey me. That was something our grandfather would do and I had sworn I would never be like him. You're the one family member I have left and, damned if I didn't repeat his mistakes." His hands framed her face. "I'm sorry, Ally. More sorry than I can tell you. And I'm so relieved and glad that you are with someone I know will never do that to you." His eyes went to JW. "Yeah, I know or can guess but I know that you love her. I know that she is safer and more loved with you than she could be with anyone else. And I know you will never hurt her or let anyone else hurt her."

Listening to David apologize to Ally, then turn and speak to him, JW felt nearly overwhelmed by the man's emotions and words. *His only family member besides Diana and Matt. Ally is nearly as precious to him as she is to me. I'm not sure I could ever say those words to a man who loved Gisele or one of the younger girls.*

"She is my life," JW said simply. "Nothing and no one else matters."

Satisfied with that, David nodded then pulled him in for a quick embrace.

"You two he-men can stay outside if you want," Diana called from the door, "but Ally and I are going to turn into popsicles in a moment."

Laughing, the three turned as JW pushed her door shut and hurried up the steps to join her. Once inside, Diana put Matt down and the boy made a beeline for Ally. Swooping him up, laughing with his baby gurgles, she cuddled him, whispering words only the two of them could hear. David took JW's jacket and, with some maneuvering, he was able to remove Ally's as Matt wrapped both his arms around her neck.

Solemn dark eyes studied him over her shoulder.

"Your daddy has given me his approval," JW told him. "Isn't that good enough for you, young man?"

A frown creased the tiny brow and a fist beat against Ally's upper back.

"Smart kid," grunted JW.

"Like his mother," David told him as Diana drew Ally down the hall.

"I'm hoping ours follows," he replied.

"Not wasting anytime," came the observation.

"I think fifteen months is enough time wasted."

Lunch was waiting in a back room that JW guessed was where the family usually ate informally. Ally started to put Matt in the highchair but he screeched and clung to her.

"I guess that settles that," she chuckled, sitting down and settling him on her lap. "We all know who's really in charge, don't we, kiddo?"

A pleased grin on his face, Matt thumped chubby fingers on the table. Her soup spoon went flying and clattered to the floor.

"At least he's sleeping through the night," sighed Diana, getting a new spoon and picking up the dirty one. "Now that we're past the first round of teething."

Sitting next to her, JW caught the expression on Ally's face.

"Are you..." she whispered.

Sending a happy smile to her husband, Diana nodded. JW wondered if he would soon have that shit-eating, ear-to-ear grin of impending fatherhood on his face.

"They say that breastfeeding is a natural birth control," Diana told her. "Well, Master Matt weaned himself just after his first birthday," in an aside to Ally, "Teeth hurt and..." With a sigh, she rolled her eyes. "His daddy did what he does best."

Ally covered Matt's ears. The other three adults laughed. Matt squawked and tugged on her fingers.

"He's too young to understand that," David teased.

"Yeah, well, I'm not," she retorted. "And what is this sudden ease talking about sex around me now?" She glanced at JW. "Or is that more of the 'he's a Dom' thing?"

"Probably," he replied.

"I'm his cousin," she complained. "Do you do that around Gisele and the girls?"

That jolted him a bit and he shuddered.

"Please, the thought of any of them—" He blinked and glanced at David. "Can you imagine Grant or Bron's reaction if anyone goes sniffing around Gisele or Heather?"

"Not to mention you," Ally laughed. "If that reaction was anything to go by."

Taking the tureen from Diana, JW placed it between Ally and himself and ladled soup into her bowl first.

"Can we change the subject?" he asked in a mild panic.

The women chuckled as Diana took two rolls from the basket and put them on Ally's bread plate. She then tore a third in half and handed it to her son. Contentedly, he gnawed on it.

"How about we discuss how much time you're going to give Diana and the women in your family to plan a wedding?" David suggested.

"Christmas Eve," Ally replied.

"What?" Diana gasped. "Ally, that's not nearly enough time—"

"You did it," she answered easily, leaning to the side to avoid spilling any of the French onion soup on Matt. "We're not waiting for a number of reasons."

Diana blinked, her gaze pinging back and forth between them before going to her amused husband. JW cut some of the mozzarella for Ally and wondered what the Englishwoman would say to that.

"Well, at least we'll be there when you say that to Mrs. Franklin," she commented.

"You can take a picture," Ally offered, grinning.

"Oh, lord," JW groaned.

****

Ally watched her cousin carefully put his son in the car seat, listening to the responses to the babbling. Glancing over at JW, she saw the intent expression on his face.

"What are you thinking?" she asked softly.

"How amazing life is," he answered, smiling. Leaning over the space between the seats, he kissed her quickly. "How lucky I am. I have you in my life. And, God willing," his eyes went to the open garage as David went around to the driver's side, "in a year, I'll be putting my child in a car seat. I never thought any of that would mean as much to me as it does."

Smiling, she simply put her hand on his thigh.

With a nod, he released the brake and took the lead in the drive to the Franklin mansion. In the time it took for the short drive, snow flurries swirled and the wind picked up.

"I don't think we'll make it back home," Ally sighed.

"Ally," JW chided, parking the SUV.

"I adore your mother, and Gisele is my best friend besides Diana, but your grandmother tries to intimidate the crap out of me."

"She does that to everyone," he told her, getting out.

With a groan, Ally got out, watching as David and Diana extricated their son and his paraphernalia. The door opened and Zoey's beaming face appeared.

"Bring that baby inside before he turns into a snowball," she scolded.

Laughing, they walked quickly to her. JW blinked when his mother hugged Ally first, then grinned as she turned to Diana and Matt. The baby babbled as JW closed the door.

"Well, I know where I stand in the pecking order," he murmured as he was finally embraced. "Where is everyone?"

"In the parlor, of course," she told him, hugging David before taking Matt. "Everyone in the family is waiting for you to introduce Ally to them officially."

"What?" Ally gasped in shock. "Everyone?"

"Mother called in everyone within a hundred-mile radius," Zoey warned her.

"Oh, God," she breathed, panting in air.

"You couldn't stop her?" JW asked, wrapping an arm around Ally.

"As if," Zoey snorted then smiled. "I called Parker and got his butt here."

"Thank you," he exhaled, glancing down at Ally. "Ready?"

"Hell, no," she muttered.

"You're not alone," Diana reminded her.

JW's fingers brushed her hip and she tilted her head. All the love and support she could ever want she found in his eyes.

"Let's do this," she stated.

"Atta girl," he smiled, guiding her to the right, where closed double doors concealed the family.

He turned the knob for the left and gave it a hard shove. Ally caught a glimpse of a crowd of people. *Dozens of them!* Gisele stood nearest the door with a tall rangy man behind her. Noting the short haircut and the way the man's eyes went to JW, Ally guessed that was Parker. Positioned in the center, with a clear space before them, stood Hal and Henrietta Franklin.

"Everyone," JW spoke up. "This is Ally Brown. A strong courageous woman who has amazingly agreed to be my wife."

Amidst the applause, he took her to his grandparents. Hal beamed and kissed her cheek.

"Welcome to the family, Ally."

"Thank you," she murmured, turning with considerable trepidation to his wife. "Mrs. Franklin."

"I think given the number of Mrs. Franklins that you should call me Grandmother," Henrietta told her, not in an entirely welcoming tone, before kissing her cheek.

"Thank you," Ally smiled. "Grandmother."

The whirl of faces and names began. While she knew a few from her generation, the brothers and their wives were a jumble. And then came the cousins.

"I think you briefly, unofficially, met Grant a couple weeks ago," JW introduced them, then winked at his cousin. "Thank God, he wanted to live in an office from the time he was about two. Took a lot of pressure off of me."

"I still can't get him to help me deal with a few people though," Grant told Ally, kissing her.

"I thought he did pretty well at that meeting," she chuckled. "I'll bet a few people at the other end of the table needed to change their pants."

"There is that," he agreed, turning to the woman at his side.

Ally had seen her at the few functions Diana had insisted she attend, but avoided being around her. The snooty, superior expression was now tinged with anger that confused Ally even as it put her on guard.

"This is my girlfriend, Sheila Jefferson," he introduced.

"Hello, Sheila," Ally smiled, offering her hand.

Ignoring the hand, cold-as-ice blue eyes narrowed.

"You bagged a Franklin," she murmured. "Well done. But how? No one even knew you were dating much less acquainted."

Her back stiffening, Ally shrugged.

"We met here at one of Grandmother's parties. As for not knowing we were dating, we preferred to keep our lives personal and not splashed across the tabloids for attention."

The anger turned to hatred and Ally knew she'd made an enemy.

"I don't recall anyone mentioning you seeing him in DC when he was wounded," sniped Sheila.

"Again, we wanted to keep that private," Ally told her, "considering everything else going on."

"Ah," Shelia murmured, her hand stroking Grant's arm as his mother joined them.

"Aunt Jackie," JW greeted her.

"Ally," the woman focused. "We're planning the calendar for next year and we need to know what to put you down for."

"Excuse me?" Ally blinked and glanced up at JW's bemused expression. *No help there.* "Put me down for what?"

"What charities do you want to take on," the emaciated woman explained. "What events?"

271

"None," replied Ally promptly with a shake of her head.

"You have to," Jackie insisted. "It's what we all do."

"I'm not going to be a society matron," Ally informed her. "We're going to be living in Connecticut and—"

"What?" Jackie interrupted. "No, dear. Franklins live—"

"JW and I will be living in Connecticut and coming to the city when David or Grant need us for business. I've already discussed things with David, and JW has been working things out with Grant this fall," Ally stated firmly. "I do not want to live here and JW supports me completely on that."

"I'll discuss that with Henrietta," Jackie told her.

"It's not for her to decide," JW said flatly.

"Nor is it for you," the older woman responded. "Come, Sheila."

Abruptly, the two women left and Ally whooshed out a breathe.

"What was all that about?" she murmured, lifting her face to see JW's expression. "Sorry."

"Why?" he frowned, his hand squeezing her shoulder. "It's what we discussed."

"You have no idea of the firestorm you unleashed," Grant told him, clearly not happy with the conversation.

"I thought you and Bron liked the idea of me moving to Connecticut," JW replied. "Both to give you a precedence for moving out and because it gave you free rein with the company."

Startled at the hint of animosity she hadn't expected, Ally caught Grant's flush. Gisele's arrival saved the moment. She pounced, flinging her arms around Ally.

"Oh, finally," she exulted, then embraced JW. "The girls and I bought every wedding magazine and book we could find so we can plan."

"Gisele," Ally tried to head her off any big plans.

"I've made an appointment for—"

"For just about everything," the man behind her interrupted dryly.

Gisele rolled her eyes even as she flushed. JW's arm left Ally as he and the man embraced with a couple back thumps.

"Ally, this is Parker Black," he told her.

"The man who brought you home," she whispered with a smile, hugging him.

"We brought each other home," Parker corrected, kissing her cheek. "And now I know who he was so determined to see so privately over Memorial weekend."

A hot flush swept over Ally and he chuckled, winking at JW. Jackie and Sheila returned, triumphant expressions on their faces as Henrietta followed them.

"What is this I hear about you not willing to be charitable?" the matriarch demanded. "And what do you mean by living in Connecticut?" Her eyes were determined and she had the air of one rarely denied.

"I'm not going to be on any charity board," Ally stated quietly, feeling JW's arm firm and steady at her waist. "I'm not going to starve myself to fit some society demand for a woman's body. And we are living in JW's home in Connecticut."

"Out of the question," she denounced. "Franklins live—"

"Grandmother," JW managed to speak.

"I have put up with a lot from my family," Henrietta interrupted. "I have done much for my family. It is not expecting too much for them to do a few simple basic things for me."

"Well, brace yourself," Ally warned her. "Because I don't follow orders well. I barely follow suggestions. I don't want to live in New York City. With few exceptions, I don't like high society people. And I'm not going to be around either unless I have to." As the matriarch's dark eyes narrowed, Ally lifted her chin. "And another thing, we're getting married on Christmas Eve."

The room had fallen silent during the conversation and her words echoed.

"My first grandchild is *not*..." She caught herself and for a moment, stared at Ally in horror. "Did you trap him?"

Ally gasped at the insinuation even as JW stepped forward.

"Grandmother, don't even go there," he cautioned.

"Well, considering your mother's behavior," she muttered. "What could we have expected? She ruined her reputation and damaged the family..."

A few steps behind her mother, Zoey jerked and Ally saw the hurt in her green eyes.

"All the more reason for us not to want to live around such judgmental people," Ally rallied. "I would rather be at JW's cabin in the woods surrounded by love than in the finest mansion because family image demanded it."

"This is intolerable," Henrietta stated, shaking her head. She gave Grant a pointed look. "At least I know your mother—"

"JW, could we leave now?" Ally asked him, turning into his embrace. "I don't care where we go, but could we leave now?"

"Abso-fucking-lutely," he told her. "David, can we stay at the penthouse?"

"Snow's gotten worse," her cousin informed him, an arm around Diana. "How about you stay with us tonight and go from there?" JW's gaze went to Parker, then back to David, who nodded. "And we have a spare room, Parker."

"Thank you," the dark-haired man replied with a nod. "It'll take me just a few minutes to pack."

His long strides took him swiftly from the room. Ally caught Gisele's pained expression and Grant's smug one. *Siblings can be so very different.*

Swallowing back his fury, JW kept his arm around Ally as he went to his mother.

"Mom?"

"She said worse the first couple years," came the whisper. "I had no idea she still felt that way."

"Zoey Elizabeth, don't be melodramatic," reprimanded her mother.

"Oh, please, Mother," Zoey shook her head. "You were horrible for years. The entire family was. The things you all said and the way you all were to me. I stayed because I thought it was better for my son to be with family. I wonder now if that was a mistake but, no," she sighed, shaking her head again. "It was necessary." Her eyes shifted to the Browns. "I don't suppose…"

"Absolutely," Diana told her. "Hurry and get what you need."

"I'll go with you," Ally spoke up.

With a grateful look, Zoey stretched out her hand. Taking it, Ally hurried out with her. In the shocked silence that caused their quick footsteps up the staircase to echo, JW looked at his grandmother who seemed stunned at what had happened.

"Grandmother, listen to me very carefully," he said quietly and firmly. "Do not say anything else unkind about my mother or my love. Ever. Do not encourage anyone else to behave that way to them, because I will know. And I don't care who the person is who said or did something, I will protect those two women with every skill I have learned and with my life."

"After everything I did for you these past few months?" the old woman demanded. "After everything the family has done? How can you—"

"After how my mother was treated?" he fired back. "It was the least you could do." Turning, he glanced about the room. "That goes for everyone here. If I think for one second that Ally or my mother are being treated with less respect than I think they deserve then I will deal with you. David, why don't you get Diana and Matt home? I'll bring Mom and Parker with Ally and me."

"Good idea," David agreed, an arm around his wife to guide her out of the room.

JW found his stoic grandfather and held the pale green eyes.

"For the first time in my life," he whispered, heard by everyone in the still silent room, "I wish I knew my father's last name so I could use it and not be a Franklin. The way my mother has been treated. The way many of you treated me and encouraged your children to do the same. The way Ally was treated just now," his gaze went to Jackie and Sheila, "this family needs to do a lot of soul searching. You are a proud lot because of family history, but what have *you* done? Have you risked everything for someone? For something? Have you been abused and stayed strong no matter what? Have you had to work your ass off to get something? No. Because everything has been handed to you on a God damned silver platter. You took because you thought it was your right. Well, guess what, people? You have money. You have position. You have power. But you sure as hell don't know a damn thing about love, compassion, or humility. God help you when you learn that lesson because some of you are so damned stiff-necked with arrogance and pride you might not survive."

With that final fling, he stomped out of the room. As he reached the bottom of the staircase, Parker appeared from the left side of the upper balcony with his battered carry-on, his sheepskin jacket over his arm. As he started down, Zoey and Ally appeared. His mother carried the garment bag she kept packed for business trips. Relieved, he went to the closet and gathered his, Ally, and his mother's coats.

"Just open the door," his mother told him, the strain breaking through her normal calm façade. "Open the door and let me get out."

Without a word, he obeyed, even as members of the family— his grandparents, uncles, Grant, Bron, and Gisele—appeared in the archway. Without looking at them, Ally's arm was around his mother's waist in silent support and comfort as they passed him, hurrying to the waiting vehicle. Parker paused beside him, ever a backup when he might need it.

JW studied them, his gaze taking in those that gathered behind them.

"Have you lived a life that will make people grieve the loss of you? Or will there be more who are glad to no longer have your hardness and judgment hanging over them?"

Turning, he nodded. Watchful eyes on the Franklins, Parker backed through the door. He only turned when JW closed it behind them. Zoey and Ally climbed into the SUV.

"I wondered what it would take," muttered Parker.

"You thought that would happen?" JW asked in surprise.

"Hell, yeah. You're not completely part of them and neither is your mother," he continued as they went around to the driver's side. "I could ask General Carruthers if he has an unmarried brother or cousin."

"Bring it up to Mom," JW told him, grinning as he suspected her answer.

They climbed in. Parker repeated his statement as JW started the engine.

"He was the two-star JW shot in the exercise on 9/11," Parker explained. "He's retired from the Reserves and is a rancher in South Dakota. One of the best men I know."

"Thank you," Zoey replied as JW released the brake and started driving. "But I think I'm too old to adapt to any man's life."

"Make him adapt to yours," Ally suggested, turning in her seat with a grin.

Zoey laughed lightly but shook her head.

"No, I think I need to figure out what my life is first. Does David have a good liquor cabinet?"

Ally winked. "The best."

"Good. I could use a stiff Scotch after that."

"Ditto," agreed Parker. "So, now what?"

"We go to David's, eat dinner, and either watch a movie or play a game," Ally suggested. "Nice and simple."

"Sounds heavenly," sighed Zoey.

Near midnight, limbs intertwined under the covers in her room, Ally reflected on what had happened.

"How did that escalate so quickly?" she wondered.

"It's how Grandmother does things," JW replied. "She'll do anything for her family as long as they stay within prescribed lines. And to keep them within the boundaries she set, she will use everything in her power to manipulate and control. Obstinance on someone else's part is not tolerated. And her daughters-in-law, especially Jackie, are her enforcers."

"And my refusing to do charity work or live in her house was outside the boundaries?"

"Oh, absolutely," he confirmed, his fingers drawing lazy circles on her upper back. "She's still not happy about Mom insisting on taking her place with the company, especially since that meant Gisele was able to take hers. She's rather old-fashioned about gender roles."

"Does that have something to do with what Alan said at the meeting?" she frowned, remembering his words.

"Everything," he answered. "Back a hundred years ago, Grandfather's grandfather reorganized the company and the family trust. The oldest of each generation is guaranteed double votes on the board, and the first four of each generation are guaranteed seats."

"Ah," she murmured. "And he didn't specify gender?"

"Nope. Mom was the first girl born in any generation who didn't have at least three or four older brothers, let alone be the oldest. After I was born, she resumed college classes in business, got her master's in finance and shocked everyone again," he drawled, making her smile, "by asserting her rights according to the trust. I think that put her brothers' backs up because they then figured she would insist I take precedent over their sons."

"As was your right," Ally pointed out.

"It was and is," he agreed. "But being stuck in an office, going over paperwork, attending meetings, and dealing with all that shit, it never appealed to me. I don't know if it does to Mom, or if she did it because she figured she'd pissed everyone off already, she might as well go all the way."

"What did you want to do?"

"I had not a clue," he admitted with a low chuckle. "I didn't want to go to college. It didn't matter how prestigious or the tradition of the family. Despite living with the family, Mom always made sure I knew I didn't have to be like them. All she wanted was for me to happy and *want* to be doing whatever I chose to do."

"How did you pick the Army?" She wondered, lifting up to see his face.

"During eleventh grade, the older brother of a classmate was accepted to West Point. I thought that a great idea, until I realized it meant four more years of sitting in a damn classroom." She giggled and he smiled. "So, I went to a recruiter, did a bunch of written tests and physical exams. I wanted to be outside, doing something that required my mind and body's full focus."

"And you do that so well inside as well," she murmured, climbing on top of him.

He smiled up at her.

"One does help the other," he agreed. "Ben Hancock wants to check out mine and Boone's land to see if he can have his men train a bit on it."

Ally nodded.

"You'd like that. Being with them. Maybe setting up trails or obstacle courses for them."

JW blinked and chuckled. His fingers threaded through her hair and brought her closer for a kiss. "You, Miss Brown, are an absolute genius. Remind me of that in the morning so I can call Ben about it."

"You don't want to call him now?" she wondered, shifting her hips over his stiffening erection.

"Hell no," he told her. "Right now, we need to practice making a baby."

His hips surged up and she moaned, rubbing her pussy against him.

"Master," she gasped.

"Come for me, love."

My stories are my way of communicating to the world..

Coming up with ideas isn't the problem. Writing them down, getting them ready for publication and then trying to get the attention of you, kind reader? That's the hard part. Well, mostly that last part. I *love* writing and am getting the hang of the formatting process. I've also really enjoyed connecting with readers through social media – especially through Instagram and TikTok. I'm still working on getting myself in front of the camera. I've been focused on getting the stories and characters out there for you to see! Those platforms have been very supportive and I've met wonderful authors and readers.

Come join in the fun!

Amazon author page – please follow for all the updates straight to your email! https://www.amazon.com/author/abbygordonauthor.com

Instagram – please join my writing journey as I try to balance writing worlds with the 'real' world – and being a human staff member to two adorable, tyrannical fluffs.

https://www.instagram.com/abbygordonauthor

Tiktok - as abbygordonauthor

If you enjoyed this story, please leave a review, maybe stop by my Instagram or TikTok pages and let me know what you liked. Thank you!

Also by the Author

Available *only* through Amazon – kindle, kindle unlimited, Vella, Paperback, Hardcover – working on audio for all

Small town, clean romance

Millboro
Coming Home – Book 1
Casanova's Heart – Book 2
Always & Forever – Book 3 *releasing November 2023*

Historical fiction

The Order of the Rose
The Hidden Rose – Book 1
Justice of the Root – Book 2
The Lost Rose – Book 3
The Heir's Redemption – Book 4 *releasing January 2024*
Tales of the Rose –
Madness of Catalan (Marco and Anna)
The Courage of the Rose (Miles)
The Honor of the Rose (the York Branch struggles to survive)

Political thriller/post-apocalyptic

The Society – Family saga — Kindle/KU only
The Ruthless – Book 1
The Defiant – Book 2
The Patriarchs – Book 3
The Promise – Book 4

Historical Romance

The Mont Verdeon Saga –
For Love and the Crown – Book 1
For a Lady's Honor – Book 2 *releasing August 18, 2023*
For the Love of a Princess – Book 3 *releasing September 22, 2023*

Erotic Romance

Love in the Shadows
First Connection – prequel novella
The Submissive's Touch

The Fall of Adonis
Thawing the Master's Heart
Find Me Sooner in the Next Life
Seduced by his Song
Enticed by his Embrace
Tempted by his Touch
The Billionaire's Fantasy – releasing February 2024 (previously published as Model Fantasy, updated)
The Vegas Virgin

Steamy fairy tale

Loves, Curses and Crowns –
      Claimed by the Beast
      Bettina's Lesson
      Hunter's Prey
      The Tower Maid
      The Tempted
      The Fury
      The Reluctant Queen

Fictional royal biography – Not Quite Royal – Part One

Available on Vella – First Three Episodes are free!

      Part of the Love in the Shadows world – erotic romance
            Second Time Lust – *publishing now*
            The Not Garden Variety series
            Petals & Thorns

      The Elements MC – erotic romance
            Claiming His – complete
            Ride of Her Life – publishing now

      The Soldier's Heart – romance – *publishing now*

      The Pineapple Express Trilogy - erotic romance *publishing now*
            Taking Pearl
            Seducing Shalla

Losing Leni

Discovering Rosie – a woman rediscovers herself during and after the pandemic – *publishing now*

Printed in Great Britain
by Amazon